PSYCHOPATHY

BOOK THREE OF THE DARK TRIAD TRILOGY

VIOLA TEMPEST

VIOLA TEMPEST PUBLISHING

CONTENTS

Prologue   1
Chapter 1   7
Chapter 2   15
Chapter 3   23
Chapter 4   31
Chapter 5   43
Chapter 6   57
Chapter 7   69
Chapter 8   79
Chapter 9   91
Chapter 10   105
Chapter 11   117
Chapter 12   129
Chapter 13   141
Chapter 14   153
Chapter 15   165
Chapter 16   175

About the Author   193
Stalk her below!   195

Raziel and Natalia stood in horror as they watched their unhinged sister. The entire Great Hall looked like it had been repainted red, and countless bodies littered the floor. As she looked around, Raziel approached Azazel slowly as she drank from a citizen's neck, and as Raziel crouched down to the level of the ungodly version of her sister, she whispered.

"Sister, what have you done?"

Azazel brought her head up from the corpse's neck as she hissed.

"The hunger."

Raziel rolled her eyes and looked back at Natalia, shaking

her head. Before Azazel could plunge back into her victim's body, Raziel snapped her fingers, causing Azazel to slump and fall unconscious.

Raziel stood up and strode over to Natalia, who was quietly walking around the room, inspecting the damage. "What can we do?" she asked.

Natalia sighed and replied, "I will see how bad the damage is in the kingdom. Can you ask around?"

Raziel nodded and quickly turned to leave the Great Hall. She walked by Azazel's body and felt sick as she saw how saturated her sister was with her kingdom's blood. Raziel felt sick to her stomach. It had been so long since she'd seen Azazel lose herself like this; she thought Azazel was finally in control of her hunger. Raziel sighed as she thought of the unnecessary death. She approached Azazel's chamber and could smell the stench of death. Raziel groaned as she opened the door and was immediately overwhelmed by the odor.

She grabbed her nose in disgust and scanned the room, looking for obvious signs, and when she found none, she walked into the room further. When she passed the couch, a glint of something caught her attention. And upon further inspection, she found that it was a latch. Raziel let go of her nose and looked closer, finding that the latch was attach to a trapdoor. She stepped aside and pulled, watching calmly as the floor fell through.

"Where do you lead?" Raziel asked out loud.

She stood up and strolled over to the bed before rummaging through the night stands. When she got to the table that was clearly on Azazel's side of the bed, Raziel was assassinated once again by the stench of decay. She looked at the floor and crouched down to look underneath the bed, and when she found nothing, she knew the smell was coming from the vent, and there was something beneath this room.

She sighed as she stood up. Her sister had been busy, and if it wasn't for a violent reason, Raziel would have been impressed. She left the bedroom and wandered the halls until she found herself in the basement—the death trail was strongest down here. Raziel came to a large room, and when she opened the door, she saw the streak of blood across the floor, and she could sense just how many men had lost their lives in this box. Fear, death, and hatred coated the entire room in a thick film, and Raziel felt heavy.

She closed the door and decided that she had seen enough to give a full report to Natalia. Leaving the basement, Raziel couldn't help but wonder how they had let it get to this point; Azazel looked like she had been spiraling for some time.

When Raziel found Natalia, she was in the garden, looking at a large portrait of an incredibly handsome man. Natalia turned to acknowledge her sister when she heard footsteps.

"The Cunning has taken place, and there was no elected winner. The projected winner took his own life after killing his opponent as some sort of political statement."

Raziel scoffed. "Why do humans always think their dramatic displays will trigger a chain of events that will end up changing the world for the better?"

Natalia softly said, "Sometimes they do. Other times, there are bigger things at play that they don't even know about. It's the price you pay as a mortal."

Raziel looked at the portrait. "He's quite handsome, isn't he?"

"Don't get your hopes up, Sister. He's dead."

"Shame." Raziel looked around the garden. "How did she get a garden this incredible?"

Natalia looked around before she answered. "I'm sure bones and blood played a big part in the growth."

The sisters left the blooming garden in silence and started to walk up the steps of the palace when Raziel said, "There's a murder chamber underneath her bedroom. It's been used several times."

Natalia sighed. "I'm not surprised. It's never a simple task with Azazel."

As Natalia began to walk faster up the stairs, Raziel sped up and asked, "What are we going to do with Azazel, Sister?"

Natalia stopped and looked at her. "The same thing we always do when she spirals. If anyone gets word of this and finds out what we're doing on Earth, you know He would send the archangels after us."

Raziel shuttered at the thought of Heaven's most ruthless soldiers.

Natalia continued, "Azazel has been off the leash for far too long, and now there are entire families who will never recover the generations lost."

Raziel agreed; Azazel *had* always been the more maniacal one. She sighed. "I'm going to move Azazel down to the chamber until she wakes up, and we can figure out what steps to take next."

Natalia nodded. "Once she's locked up, head back to the compound. I'm going to stay here for a while longer to try and salvage what I can of the kingdom."

1

After the fall, Raziel only had one thing on her mind: love. Every time she finished a cycle on Earth, the idea of *love* intrigued her. She had seen hundreds of plays and movies based on love, read countless books and poems describing the feelings that people have when they are falling for their heart's desire, and it sounded like the next best thing to Heaven, in Raziel's ears. While her sisters were looking for praise and power, Raziel wanted to retire on a plot of land and dive deeper into the world of love.

Nirvana was created when Raziel fell, the compound built on the holiest land in the depths of the Amazon rainforest. For the longest time, it was just Raziel preparing the compound. She sustainably built small cabins, large gardens, and greenhouses. By the time she had completed her work, the compound became an environmentally-sustainable oasis, and when she was pleased, Raziel slept for several weeks after.

Over time, word traveled by mouth that there was a community welcoming anyone looking to break free from societal norms and wanting to embrace their inner flame. People from all over the world came in search of free love. They lived in harmony with the other tribes that lived in the forest's depths, and had a strong relationship with the animals that called the jungle their home. In all her years of existence, Raziel had never felt the type of peace that she felt when the walls of Nirvana were erected.

While the people were free to come and leave as they pleased, once they felt the sense of community and the warm embrace of true freedom, no one wanted to. They lived their days working on the land, singing and dancing in the rain, and engaging in bacchanals that would cause Caligula to blush. There was no hatred, no despair, and no one ever needed to ask for anything because everything was already provided.

Raziel treasured her community and tried to shut off her thoughts before she landed on Earth. Whenever she thought of her sisters, a pang of guilt pulled at her heart; she knew they could only stay apart for so long before the darkness took over them. Over the years, Natalia stopped requesting that Raziel come to help immobilize Azazel, which was ideal for Raziel. Azazel's hunger scared her, and the damage she could cause left some of the deepest trauma that Raziel had ever experienced.

The Nirvana commune had fallen into a comfortable routine, one that Raziel was prepared to live with for the rest of eternity. Everyone was in love with each other and cared about the safety and well-being of the commune, doing their part to keep the balance. Once a week, they gathered together in Raziel's hut to talk about religious theology and discuss how their belief system could change the world for the better. Raziel taught lessons in free love and being one with nature, appreciating everything from the smallest creatures to things that seemed insignificant, like boulders or small pebbles.

While things were mainly foraged from the jungle and their own gardens, there were certain supplies that were needed from town. Once a month, a select few would venture into the closest city to get enough supplies for their pantry.

The city didn't bother them, and they didn't bother the city. While they walked the streets, they would busk to raise more money for their groceries and spread Raziel's message of free love. By the end of their visit, however, people were usually ready for them to go back into the jungle, although after some time, the locals were unable to pinpoint exactly where in the jungle they had come from.

While they were in the city, Raziel wouldn't worry about them and would sleep until they were back within the walls; they had all become so close that when they were gone, she felt like a part of herself was missing, a part she could only find in sleep. The night they returned, a large feast would take place, and they would celebrate the departed members' return for days. The commune was everything that Raziel wanted in life; she felt the most content when she was tangled up with her loves.

The only thing she couldn't ignore was the small and empty feeling in the deepest part of her body, and while she did feel love, Raziel always thought that she experienced it in a different way than the humans in her care did. Angels were created to carry out orders, not feel emotions, and regardless of how much she tried, Raziel couldn't fall in love with anyone. She just didn't feel connected to them.

With each passing year, the feeling became harder to ignore. She eventually reached a point in her leadership where she wanted to enforce rules that would benefit the entire community. Raziel saw how large the group was getting and knew that to maintain order, boundaries were a necessity. When gathered the community together in her cabin and laid the rules out, which included prohibiting violence, negativity, and monogamy.

Raziel came to the conclusion that because access to every person in the community was open, there wasn't a need for monogamy, and Raziel had gone through enough violent situations during her time of being on the front line of Heaven's most loyal defenders.

The Nirvanians were welcoming and open to the rules and had abided by them for centuries. The one thing that Raziel *wasn't* prepared for was the sting she felt when members of the community died. It left holes in her heart, and even when new members came looking for their Nirvana experience, it still wasn't enough to repair the woe that she felt for every lover she'd lost. While Raziel tried for millennia to fall helplessly and deeply in love, regardless of what she did, she could never achieve the exact feeling that she had always dreamed about. Most of the time, she just felt numb.

If she had it her way, she would have been forgotten. Raziel always felt like the responsibility of being an angel was too much, and rarely enjoyed going to Earth with her sisters. It always turned into some sort of battle, and by the time Raziel fell, she was beyond ready to leave Heaven and the tyranny that came with it. And while her sisters needed time to understand and cope with the Creator's decision, Raziel thrived in her exile.

And even when new people coming in to the compound became a rarity, she had grown to appreciate the community she had and realized that they were worth their weight in gold. They had all fallen into a comfortable way of living. Everyone played their part, and Raziel kept intruders and malicious characters away from the compound with an invisible barrier around the outskirts. It cloaked the community from any sort of scanning devices, satellites, and even signals would be lost if explorers got too close.

It had gotten back to Raziel that locals had started to refer to their corner of the forest as the fauna *Devil's Triangle*. This brought Raziel much relief; it meant that people wouldn't look for a third fallen angel in case her sisters were ever discovered and overpowered. Over the years, Raziel stopped thinking of her sisters and focused on her own world. The longer she was on Earth, the less she cared about a search party coming for her or for her divinity. Eventually, people stopped wanting to leave, and babies started being born within the walls of Nirvana.

It truly *did* take a village to raise a child, and that's exactly what conspired. Raziel cherished every baby as if the infant were her own, and ensured that both the mother and child had everything they needed—plus more—to achieve the highest quality of life in the community.

At first, Raziel had concerns about the men in the community. But then she came to realize that all the men who had journeyed to Nirvana were a different breed of man, more in touch with their feminine side and did the work to close the toxic masculinity wound that so often took over men's lives. Each man cared for the children and allowed the women to heal themselves both physically and mentally. It was better than Heaven; it was a new kind of bliss, and Raziel wished that her sisters could have stayed and enjoyed it with her.

Raziel was brought out of her daydream by the sound of a ringing bell. She looked around and realized that she had been so deeply entrenched in her memories that she had completed the entire potato harvest without even paying it any attention. She smirked, pleased with her work. She turned to the baskets and picked them up to bring them inside. When she got closer, she heard her people singing, singing their praise and gratitude for her bringing them all together, for her choosing Earth over Heaven, and for her wanting Nirvana to rival Heaven in every way.

The people here experienced a love like nothing else, and they were in constant awe of her and what she could offer them in terms of leadership. They had their own beliefs in the commune; they didn't pray to the god that banished Raziel and her sisters. No, after years of restructuring the humans in her care, Raziel taught them to give thanks to the Universe, thanking the cosmos for blessing them with her and guiding them to Nirvana.

Even though she didn't need any kind of nourishment, the prayers revitalized any depleted energy, and Raziel felt ready to face her family, the people who made Nirvana otherworldly and truly a better Heaven. She walked through the large doors and greeted the community. They all erupted into thunderous applause when she walked to the front of the large room, waving at everyone and greeting anyone who ran up to her. The children ran around her in excitement and tried to pull her to where they were sitting. Even though she had never felt the deepness of being helplessly in love with someone, this type of love had its own kind of magic and was something Raziel would be eternally grateful for.

She looked around the room, trying to make eye contact with as many people as she could. Once the parents came to collect their children, she continued to the front of the crowd and held her hands up to signal that she wanted to speak. Raziel began explaining the upcoming harvest for the full moon that was due the following week. She explained that the adults would be partaking in their monthly moon ritual, and that the children were expected to be in bed and asleep long before then. Raziel made sure to wink at the small children, causing them to all start giggling in excitement and call out for her. Once they quieted down, Raziel mentioned that the wall at the south end of the compound looked like it was leaning, and immediately, several members of the group volunteered at once to fix it, making Raziel's heart swell with pride.

2

They all said a final prayer, and Raziel gave her blessing for everyone to begin their meals while she gathered her own plate and filled it before going to sit at one of the tables that had space for her. When she settled in, one of the members at the table—who worked in the kitchen—brought up that the pantry was starting to get low again. Raziel furrowed her brow, trying to remember the last time she had sent a scavenging crew into the city.

Once she had swallowed her food, she asked, "When was the last time we went into town?"

The kitchen hand, Ramona, replied, "Approximately six months ago."

Raziel nodded. "Okay, get a group of five people together and leave tomorrow afternoon. We will move some things around and ensure that you're prepared."

Ramona nodded and asked, "What about the ritual?"

Raziel paused for a brief moment before she replied with a question of her own. "Do you think you'll be able to get everything we need in five days?"

Ramona looked around the table. "You think we'll be able to get *six months* of rations in five days?"

Raziel kept eating as if she didn't hear Ramona's question. Several minutes later, Raziel calmly said, "Ramona, if you feel like you're going to fail, you will. If you feel like you'll succeed, you will. If you want to get the proper amount of rations in the shortened time to make it back for the ritual, you will." She stood up and looked around the table. "I trust that you'll all be able to sort this out amongst yourselves."

Raziel walked through the aisles between the tables and stopped to talk to those who needed to. When she reached a table where several very pregnant women were eating fresh fruit, she stopped and took a seat.

"Hello, my vessels. How are we feeling today?" Raziel reached out and gently cupped the swollen belly of the woman beside her.

The woman smiled and inched closer to Raziel. "She's strong. She was kicking earlier." The woman moved Raziel's hands to where she felt the flutters earlier, as if the unborn baby sensed her. It wasn't very long before Raziel felt the small kicks of the life growing inside.

This caused Raziel to frown, and she looked up at the woman to say, "You're right, she *is* strong." Raziel continued to ask each woman how they were feeling and if they needed anything. Each one declined her offer until she got to the end of the table, where a blonde woman—who was approaching her due date very quickly—was avoiding eye contact.

Raziel approached her and grabbed her hand as she sat down beside her. "My sweet, beautiful Lily. What's wrong?"

Lily looked embarrassed. "I have been feeling… something. For the past day or so."

"You didn't tell anyone?"

Lily shook her head sheepishly. "I didn't want to worry anyone. I was sure that it was just gas or something, but I'm afraid the closer you came to me, the stronger the feelings have become."

As she finished her sentence, Lily let out a cry of pain, and Raziel recognized it at once. She looked around to find the midwife and instructed her to ready the birthing cabin. The expecting mothers all stood up as Raziel helped Lily from the table. As she stood, there was a wet *whooshing* sound, followed by the sound of it splattering all over the floor. Lily's water broke, and Raziel smiled. Lily looked up in fear. It was her first birth, and Raziel reassured her that she would be just fine as she guided her out of the dining hall.

They slowly walked the path to the birthing cabin that was tucked away in the quietest part of Nirvana. With every contraction, Raziel guided Lily through the pain with breathing exercises, and Lily cried out in pain as the contractions started to become increasingly aggressive. When they reached the cabin, Raziel opened the door to reveal a tranquil space, complete with a birthing pool, a view of the forest with the sun poking through the spaces between the branches, candles everywhere, and the sound of a harp being played from the corner of the cabin, giving a new meaning to serenity.

"Lily, you are about to embark on the most divine journey that any birth-giver can go on." Lily groaned, and Raziel quietly said, "Give yourself over to the pain, Lily. Birth is natural, and your body knows what to do. Stop fighting your body and let go."

Lily bobbed her head, and she asked through gasps, "Will it take long?"

Raziel and the midwife, Lorena, exchanged looks, and Lorena jumped in. "The first one usually takes the longest, but it's the perfect time to connect with your foremothers and feel what each of them went through to bring each new person into the world. Ride the waves and give thanks to the Universe for providing you the opportunity to experience it."

Lily screamed, "I need drugs!"

Raziel remained calm, and Lorena replied, "It will be a long night if you think like that." She helped Raziel lead Lily over to the sitting area. There were books, toys, and other things to help relieve pain without any kind of pharmacological interference.

Raziel had faith in Lorena. She had over twenty years of midwife experience, and she even worked in the city's emergency department for ten years before that.

It had been several hours of labor contractions when Raziel heard a knock on the door. When she opened it, she was relieved to see that Ramona had brought a platter filled with food, and glasses with a pitcher of ice chips. Raziel graciously thanked her and brought everything inside to cut down on outside contamination until *after* the baby was born.

She brought the tray over and set it on the small table. She then put together a glass full of ice chips for Lily, who was now lying naked on the couch, covered only by a translucent sheet. When Raziel handed Lily the glass, it slipped through Lily's fingers and shattered all over the floor. Raziel looked at Lorena, who had a concerned look on her face and shook her head.

"The baby is breech," Lorena suddenly said when she took a look under the sheet.

Raziel shook her head and asked, "What do we do?"

Lorena ran her hand through her hair and replied, "I need to turn the baby around." She sheepishly looked at Raziel. "We need to sedate her. It's the humane thing to do; it's already too much stress on the baby and on Lily."

"It's your call, Lorena. It's what you're here for. Do your job."

Lorena jumped to action and rushed to the door. "I am going to the infirmary to get what we need. Keep Lily calm; that's the key here."

As she ran out the door, Lily watched her and desperately asked, "Where is she going?"

Raziel rushed to Lily's side, paying no attention to the glass shards all over the floor. She started to pat Lily's forehead to get rid of the sweat starting to form, and she noticed that Lily's breathing was shallow and her eyes were darting around the room.

Raziel started to speak in a soothing voice. "Lily, your baby is breech," she began. This caused Lily to sit up, and before she could panic, Raziel put her hand over Lily's chest, and as her hand started to glow, she looked deep into Lily's eyes and said, "Lily, you're going to be just fine. We are going to sedate you so you don't feel anything, but you need to stay calm. It's important that you control your breathing and focus on having a new baby soon." She raised her hand from Lily's chest, and Lily leaned back, her breaths slowing and her body slumping in relaxation.

When Lorena came back, Lily was almost asleep. Raziel was cleaning up the broken glass and ice, and made sure it was clear for Lorena to walk over. Lorena was able to administer the sedative, and as Lily began to drift off, Lorena quickly turned the baby back around and got Lily back on track, checking every half hour to ensure that the baby didn't turn around again.

Just as the sun was beginning to rise—while the moon

was faintly still in the sky—a healthy baby girl came into the world, loudly announcing her arrival. Lily fell back, exhausted, as her body gave one final push. Raziel was the one to cut the umbilical cord and placed the freshly washed baby on her mother's chest.

Once the mother and child were wrapped up in warm blankets, Raziel approached Lily and asked, "What name have you decided on?"

Lily smiled and looked at the perfect new addition she held in her arms. "Oriana."

"It's beautiful; *she* is beautiful."

Raziel slipped out of the cabin, filled with a renewed sense of hope. She always found so much pride in herself watching babies being born, knowing this was all her doing. A new generation of Nirvanians filled Raziel with the love she so desired that she stopped missing Heaven when she figured out how much Earth had to offer her.

3

As Raziel walked through the field toward her cabin, she braced herself for the morning and what it offered her. The dew drops on the grass glistened, and the birds started to sing through the trees beyond the wall. It was a beautiful day to be born, and Raziel thought that a bouquet of flowers for Lily and Oriana would be the *perfect* way to welcome Oriana to Nirvana. It never brought her much joy. Nothing really ever did, except for true love, but she did it anyway.

She plastered on a straight face as she opened the door to her home. Her cabin. It was just small enough for her and contained a simple sitting area, a place to brew tea, and a large canopy bed at the back of the cabin that was surrounded by several large potted Monstera plants, soaking up the early morning sun. Raziel treasured her simple life and thrived on minimalism, unlike her overindulgent sisters.

Raziel threw her long blonde hair up into a messy bun on top of her head and secured her hair with two sticks that she made from a pair of branches found on the ground. When she looked at the small reflective mirror in front of her, she was pleased with her appearance and became excited to break the news of Oriana's arrival to the rest of the community.

When Raziel left her cabin, she stopped by her personal rose garden and picked the most beautifully-bloomed roses for Lily and Oriana. When she had a large bouquet of flowers, she continued toward the Main Hall, where the community would be waiting for their daily schedule. When Raziel rounded the corner to the front of the building, she was greeted by the sound of people whispering excitedly, and when they saw her, they stopped, and it felt like they were holding their breath as Raziel smiled widely and announced.

"It's a girl!" The community erupted in applause and celebration. "Today, we will be celebrating Oriana's birth with a grand feast… and also the departure of our foraging crew."

She looked to Ramona, who nodded, acknowledging that a crew had been procured. Raziel nodded back and dismissed everyone, looking forward to bringing them all together again and introducing Oriana to them all.

Raziel continued to the kitchen to get a glass vase for the bouquet. When she found one, she filled it with water and placed the flowers inside of it. After fluffing some of the blooms, Raziel made a simple breakfast for Lily, including fresh fruit with lots of chia and hemp seeds. It was the *perfect* meal to replenish Lily after the hard work she did the night before.

She gathered everything she needed, placed them on a platter, and walked out the back door to avoid anyone stopping her and prolonging Lily from eating. When she approached the birthing cabin again, she was overwhelmed with a sense of peace and optimism for the future. Oriana was the future of the compound, and Raziel knew that everyone in the community would work hard to ensure that she had the best possible upbringing.

When Raziel opened the door to the cabin, the inside was saturated with sunshine and peacefulness. Lily and Oriana were snuggling in bed at the back of the cabin. As Raziel approached the pair, she saw that Oriana was sleeping, and she was able to get a better look at the beautiful bundle. Her cheeks were plump, and her little thumb was brought up to her mouth as her eyes squeezed shut.

The look on Lily's face was one of gratitude when she saw what Raziel had in her hands. She mouthed her thanks as Raziel rested the platter near her and backed away again, trying to leave as quietly as possible. Before she left the cabin, she blew them a kiss and took the scene in once more. Raziel had never wanted children more than when she saw new babies being held by their mothers, still fresh to the world.

As she closed the door behind her, she heard her name being called, and she turned around to see a group of people walking toward her. She waved and started to sprint toward them.

When they met halfway across the field, one of the men, Troy, came forward and told her that there was a problem with the garden. Raziel's face darkened as she replied, "I was just there yesterday and saw nothing wrong."

Troy exchanged looks with the other people in the group and continued, "It looks like everything is now frozen. Half of the garden is ruined."

Raziel shook her head in disbelief. "That's impossible. It doesn't frost in Nirvana. I'll take a look, but stop wasting my time with nonsense."

She dismissed the group and turned her attention to the large garden. When she approached the closest fruit trees and saw that they were indeed in rough shape, Raziel felt a strong shiver shoot up her spine. She paused and closed her eyes, relying on her other senses to weed out the intruder. Whatever it was, it was powerful enough to radiate through the barrier.

When she didn't feel anything, she focused back on the garden, and when she opened her eyes, the garden was back to its original lush and beautiful state. Raziel looked around at the garden and couldn't help but feel a bit uncomfortable. She quickly harvested some peaches to bring to the kitchen. When she walked into the industrial kitchen, it was quiet, and the community members were all circled around the island. Raziel brought the fresh fruit over and placed the basket down on the island.

"There's nothing wrong with the garden," she simply stated.

But then one of the chefs in the compound stepped forward and replied, "Troy told us that there wouldn't be any fruits or vegetables today."

Raziel raised a brow, and she sternly asked, "Is that so?" She tapped her fingernails on the hard surface. "Well, I guess Troy knows better than I do. And if any of you dare to agree with him over your leader, well, you're free to leave at any time."

She left the kitchen, fists clenched and brows furrowed, as she left her humans behind in shock. She rushed to the back part of Nirvana, which housed a large body of water that was home to fresh salmon and other types of crustaceans. As she got closer to the flowing stream, her frustration started to lessen, and with every glimmer of the shiny scales, Raziel returned to her peaceful demeanor.

Once she felt like she was back to normal, she backed away from the water. And when she turned around, she saw several of the community members hanging back. Raziel took a deep breath and realized that she had overreacted, though she still felt no sympathy for those behind her. The group all exchanged nervous looks when she approached them, and one of the members stepped forward.

Raziel stared at her for a minute before reaching out a hand. "What do you want, Sarah?"

Sarah cleared her throat and said, "The foraging team is preparing to leave. Ramona is eager to get everything stocked and back in time before the full moon."

"I'll be there shortly." Raziel strolled away from the group and went to sit down beside the water.

The group backed away from her, and as they walked away, Raziel could hear them mumbling amongst themselves but couldn't make out what they were saying. She focused on the sounds of the rushing water, the frogs in the distance, and the birds flying overhead.

When she finally felt grounded, Raziel let out a slow breath and felt herself finally relaxed. Standing up, she started to slowly walk to the gates, where all the village people had gathered to bid their farewell. She forced a smile on her face and approached them, and the closer she got, the quieter they became. Humans were shifting uncomfortably, and she could feel her agitation start to bubble.

What a bunch of pathetic weaklings...

Raziel tried to keep her emotions in check when she saw Ramona in the center of the group, shaking hands and exchanging departing words. When she spotted Raziel, Ramona broke away from the crowd and dropped to her knees in front of her leader, and she cautiously whispered, "I hope you don't mind. I moved things up because I wanted to ensure that we had enough time. I didn't want to disturb you."

Raziel sighed and crouched down in front of her most faithful follower, cupped her face in her hands, and she quietly whispered back, "Ramona, you have my blessing. Just don't screw it up." She stood up and pressed her hands together in prayer. "Please join me in a silent prayer for our brave foragers. May they return safely and with abundance."

The entire compound turned quiet as they all prayed. Raziel could feel the energy radiating off of the crowd, and she felt the overwhelming vibration of their prayers drifting into the Universe. She took a deep breath, feeling it nourish her entire being. She was lucky that all she needed to sustain her divinity was the energy that humans offered to the Universe when they prayed.

Once she felt like she was ready, she broke the silence. "Now get out of here. We'll all die if you don't." Raziel hollered at the foragers. Nervous chuckles erupted through the crowd, and Raziel watched them leave the large gates. She turned to the rest of the commune and loudly asked, "Shall we have a bonfire tonight? We have a new addition to welcome." She felt like something was off. Typically, the commune would share a last meal with the group before they left. Perhaps Ramona figured that with Raziel's mood, it would be best to leave sooner.

Raziel sighed at the thought of Ramona. She had been a part of the community for twenty years, coming to Nirvana as a bright-eyed teenager after running from an abusive household. Raziel had welcomed her with open arms and stepped into the maternal role that Ramona needed. In return, Ramona had shown nothing but dedication and faith to Raziel and her dreams of Nirvana's evolution. Ramona was the one community member whom Raziel could trust wholeheartedly; she was the only one to lead the excursion into the modern world.

As Raziel crossed the field again, she changed directions to go check on the garden once more. She wanted to be sure that things were indeed healthy, and perhaps, she had just been seeing things from the lack of sleep.

When she reached the garden, she was pleased to see that everything was overflowing with growth again. She picked up a big, juicy tomato and was surprised by the size of it. But her mind was still confused from the morning's occurrence. She knew what she had seen, and other members of the community had seen the same thing.

4

It didn't make sense to her and was something that Raziel couldn't ignore. The entire time she had been in Nirvana, they never had anything but sunshine and the perfectly-timed rainstorm. She looked around her and noticed that none of the community members were anywhere near her. She then looked up at the sun's position and realized that they were probably all in the dining hall. Putting the tomato in her pocket, Raziel left the garden and walked toward the entrance.

As she got closer, she heard the hum of conversation, and a small smirk crept upon her face. Raziel knew she had some wounds to heal. These people depended on her to remain stable and level-headed; lashing out at them just reiterated that she wasn't above human emotions. She couldn't let them think that she had any sort of humanity in her; she had spent too much time convincing them that she was indeed a fallen angel.

Raziel was thrown back into memories of the early days of Nirvana. To convince the first generation of the commune members to join her, she had to spawn a magnificent rose garden before their very eyes to prove her divinity. She relished in the memory of the shocked smiles on her followers' faces. They had all dropped to their knees, asking for her forgiveness, treating her as if she were the Messiah himself, while she thrived on their love and the energy that they radiated.

But she also knew that she would be struck down if she continued with that narrative. Instead, she told the humans about her time in Heaven, and how she and her sisters wanted the people on Earth to have free will and to advance mankind so they wouldn't rely on the Creator so much. When the humans heard this, they became angry with the god whom they had prayed to, and they immediately renounced their faith in Him and followed Raziel instead. However, right now, she wasn't proving herself to be much better. She needed to make things right again. She *had* to gain their trust back.

When she walked into the hall, it turned silent instantly. Raziel felt her face fall, and she walked to the front of the room, feeling everyone's eyes on her. When she turned around to face them, she felt as if a spotlight was on her. Raziel cleared her throat and forced another smile as she looked around, trying to make eye contact with as many people as possible.

"I feel like I need to be open with all of you." She watched as people looked around. "This morning, I was a lesser form of myself. I had a poor reaction to something that I didn't understand, and truthfully, I *still* don't understand." She saw Troy in the back of the room perk up as she continued. "The garden that morning really *did* look like it had been overtaken by frost. Troy didn't lie when he said that there wouldn't be any fruits and vegetables. I don't know exactly what happened between his check and mine, but when I had gone to inspect it, everything had returned to normal." She pulled the tomato out of her pocket, and the crowd murmured at the beauty of the fruit.

Raziel looked around and asked, "Will someone sacrifice their knife for a moment?" Several people rushed toward her, and she took a knife from a burly-looking man. She walked over to the closest table and gathered the crowd around her. "See, everything is just fine," she said as she sliced the tomato in half, expecting the plush red flesh to appear before her.

Instead, the inside was black and rotten! There were dozens of maggots pushing their way through the fruit. Raziel recoiled in disgust, and everyone gasped at the scene. Raziel looked around, and then back at the tomato in confusion. She stepped closer to it, and as everyone gathered around to get a better look, she had no answers.

Troy quickly came up to the front and stood beside her. "I don't know how this could've happened. It's like the Garden of Eden here," he said cautiously, and she glared at him.

"Never mention that place here!" she hissed, catching those close enough to hear off-guard.

Troy stared at his leader, and his voice dropped. "I am so sorry. I didn't realize there were prohibited terms." His mouth went into a straight line as he challenged her with his sarcastic words.

Raziel came closer to him. "That place has *nothing* on Nirvana. It's an insult to even begin to compare the two, and you will be sure to remember that." She gripped his arm and dug her nails straight into his skin, piercing just deep enough to get the message across. Troy gasped as Raziel brought him to her face, and she whispered, "Can you come to my cabin tonight? We have some things to discuss, one-on-one."

She smirked at him and released his arm as he nervously sputtered, "Yes, I think it's best if we discuss it privately."

Raziel looked back at the tomato. It had been a while since she'd seen anything like this, and it could only mean a few things—all of which were detrimental to their quiet way of life.

She took a deep breath and bellowed, "Perhaps we just need to move the garden! The soil may be tainted from producing so many wonderful things for us, all of which we should be grateful for. Perhaps we could say a prayer thanking the Earth for doing its work and providing us with the things we need to nourish our bodies properly."

Everyone began to whisper amongst themselves. Raziel could feel her frustration starting to creep up again. She clapped her hands loudly, and everyone's necks instantly snapped to look at her. In a calming voice, she said, "We are all going to carry about our days. We are going to move the garden to the east side of the compound. Thank the Earth for its service, and then we are going to celebrate the birth of Oriana. Is that clear?"

The crowd all nodded at the same time, none of them blinking or moving. Raziel grabbed the tomato and chucked it out of the closest window. She clapped her hands together loudly again and announced, "Let's eat!"

When she walked over to the serving table, she saw Troy staring at the spot where the tomato had been. Raziel could see that he was trying to figure out what had happened. She knew there would be a mental gap for everyone, but as long as they went back to normal and the whispering stopped, that's all she cared about.

Raziel grabbed a plate and made her way down the line to get her vegetarian macaroni. She then went over to a table at the back of the usually empty hall. It had a view of the forest behind the compound. As she sat down, she saw a flock of birds flying out of the trees. She ate in silence as she scanned the area, looking for other signs of what might have happened. Raziel felt her body tense, as if she were expecting something to happen or someone to come crashing through the wall.

Before she realized it, her plate was empty, and she stood up. As she turned around, most of the people had already left. Raziel was relieved that no one had approached her while she was deep in thought. She came to the conclusion that perhaps she needed to take a bit of downtime. Her grounding from earlier hadn't taken, and she realized that it had been more than a day since she had gotten any real sleep.

Walking away from the table, Raziel said to the closest kitchen worker, "Can you ensure that a full plate gets over to the birthing cabin? I bet our new mother needs something to fill her belly."

With a smile, the worker nodded enthusiastically. "Absolutely, I will deliver it myself!"

As Raziel walked to her own cabin, a loud crash got her attention, and she looked in the direction that it came from, pleased to see that the garden was being ripped up, and the surrounding gates and fences were being brought down. She was always impressed with the speed at which things were accomplished in Nirvana. The people who lived here were something remarkable.

When she opened the door to her cabin, she was met with the overwhelming scent of roses, feeling completely relaxed. She looked around at the soft light coming in through the windows and the serene setting, realizing that this was *exactly* what she needed. She walked across the room and threw herself face-first onto the bed.

She was asleep by the time she even hit the bed and fell into a dream that felt incredibly familiar. Raziel roamed the forest after landing on Earth, calling for her sisters with no response. She felt alone and like her search efforts were pointless. She called for God, begging for forgiveness, crying for Him and His light.

As she moved her shoulders, she screamed out in pain. The places where her wings once rested were now ugly, raised scars, but the excruciating agony from having her wings ripped from her was her only companion. Knowing that she could never return to the Kingdom of Heaven left her feeling lost and dark. As the sun fell, Raziel's fear increased with every crackle of leaves and snapping of twigs. She felt like she was being watched as she walked deeper into the forest, hoping to come across her sisters or someone who could help her.

When no one came to save her, and her sisters wouldn't answer, Raziel finally understood that she was all alone. She collapsed to her knees and let out a monstrous cry. Any animals that were around her quickly left the area, knowing that they were in the presence of something otherworldly.

The scene quickly morphed into a dark time. It had been about fifty years since the fall. The land started to rot, and the food tasted like ash. Raziel was summoned to help her sister after years of unanswered calls. They had come to the realization that one of the Creator's cruel punishments was that while they rested and kept each other's divinity in balance, if one slipped and started to take too much from Earth and from the cosmos, the other two would suffer for the shortcomings of the third. The kingdoms would wither, and they would lose their powers until they were able to come together to balance their divinity again.

The image of Azazel's face gushing blood and the countless bodies piled up while her hunger still wanted more was enough to wake Raziel up. She sat up and looked around, expecting to see blood covering both the walls and her own body, with an estranged look on a face standing beside her. When she realized that she was alone, Raziel sighed in relief.

It had been so long since she had dreamt of her sisters, of their fall, and of the newfound punishments they now had to live with. She sat up and rubbed her head, knowing that it was coming. Azazel's hunger would *never* be squashed, and it was almost due for another reset. Raziel let out a groan when she thought of Azazel. In Heaven and in her service, hunger had never been something they had to deal with.

They weren't exactly sure what initiated the insatiable need, but when they finally figured out that she needed to be stopped, Azazel had taken out the majority of her kingdom, only leaving six families, and even then, they were thinned out. The first time, they made her sleep for a hundred years so the kingdom could replenish itself. Raziel and Natalia took turns checking in with the kingdom and made the decisions that needed to be made. Azazel still had no recollection of that ever happening; she thought she only slept for one night, which worked in everyone's favor.

Raziel stood up; she hated thinking of her sisters and the responsibility that came with being divine beings on Earth. Part of her wished that they had just followed orders and stayed in Heaven. She looked around her cabin, aggravated that her dreams had been plagued by Azazel.

She decided that she needed to rest longer that night and look for a medicinal solution, knowing that if another reset was coming, she would need to be as rested as possible. She changed into a flowy bright yellow dress, figuring that the bright color would help brighten her day and help her get into a celebratory mood.

She walked out of the cabin and could see that a giant pyramid of wood was built for the bonfire. Raziel felt her heart start to warm and become overwhelmed with love when she thought of Oriana's entrance into the world. It was so raw and was one of the only times they were able to tap into their divine powers, and she was always so intrigued by it.

As she approached the pyramid, she heard her name being called. She turned around to see Troy coming toward her, and he was walking with quite a bit of speed.

When he got close enough, he roughly asked, "Where have you been?"

Raziel's brow furrowed, and she replied, "None of your business. What do you want, Troy?"

Troy bowed. "I've just noticed that you're rarely around to help with the heavy lifting, and I need to be honest. It's kind of a crappy personality trait to have. Laziness."

Raziel turned her head slowly and titled it, finding the right words. "Laziness? I built this entire compound before your parents were even born, before your family even immigrated here, by myself, getting it ready, perfect!" Her tone became harsh and sharp, causing Troy to look around. She took a step closer and whispered, "Come with me, Troy. I think it's time we solve this issue once and for all. Don't you?"

He anxiously nodded, following her as she turned to go back into the cabin. She led him past the small building and into the rose garden. He looked around. "I have never been back here before."

Raziel smirked. "I tend to keep this place for myself, my own oasis within an oasis." She motioned around her and continued, "I have a secret to getting these magnificent roses. Would you like to know how?" She glared at him.

If he had looked at her instead of inspecting the roses, he

would have seen the psychotic look that had taken over her face. When Troy finally looked back at her, Raziel put her hand on his forehead and gripped both sides of his head. She began to absorb his life force, and the more she took, the more his body shrunk down to bones, and eventually, Troy became a shell of what he used to be.

Once the body collapsed to the ground, Raziel shivered as her body was replenished, and she felt as if she was new again. She quickly looked around, and when she realized that she was alone, she promptly dug up several of the rose bushes to reveal numerous dried-out, decomposing bodies inside the hole.

Raziel rolled Troy's husk into the hole and covered it with dirt and the rose bushes again. Once she was satisfied with her work, she quickly watered all of the roses and walked out of her garden. Her hair had become incredibly shiny, and her skin looked supple and youthful. She had forgotten the vitality that the human life force gave her. She hated killing humans; she loved all of them, but some just weren't capable of change and were more valuable as fertilizer for her rose garden instead of being released back into the outside world.

She knew she would need to come up with a story. There were many people who were with Troy up until he came to find her, knew that she was going to be the last to see him, and Raziel knew that questions would be raised.

When she saw the group outside of the dining hall, her worries subsided; they all loved her and would believe whatever she told them. They had also seen Troy challenge her repeatedly and would undoubtedly support her in whatever choice she made. Raziel could simply tell them that Troy opted to leave the commune, and she'd supported his choice, given they had been butting heads the last several days. She knew they would believe her and move on from their grief of never seeing Troy again.

Raziel smirked as she got closer to the crowd, and one of them noticed her approaching. They reached for her and pulled her into the middle of the group. Music began to play from behind them, and they all started dancing, giving their thanks to the Universe for the safe arrival of a new generation at Nirvana. The party went on late into the night, good food had been prepared, and everyone ate their fill, danced until their legs went weak, and laughed until their throats were raw. Raziel always loved these celebrations; it showed how much love humans were capable of, and would erase any knowledge of the horrible things that they were more likely to do if given a chance for a short amount of time.

When the new mother and baby had retired for the evening, the celebration took a deliciously wicked turn. Raziel got lost in the sea of caresses and fevered kisses until the first sun rays crept across the compound. When she opened her eyes, she felt at peace with the world and felt like she was surrounded by an impenetrable wall of love. Just as she'd always wanted.

5

As Raziel lifted arms and legs off of her, she quietly giggled, amused at how deep her lovers always slept afterward. She stood up and quietly walked away from the pile of people cuddling near the bonfire. As she approached the kitchen, the birds started to sing their morning tunes, and a light breeze brushed against her naked body. Raziel felt free. Any lingering regret about Troy had disappeared into the night.

She walked over to her head chef and kicked him hard. "Get up," she hissed. "The people need breakfast."

The chef quickly scurried up off the floor and rushed into the kitchen, throwing together a mountain of fruit and pancakes, which Raziel quickly snatched away from him. As she brought it out to the serving area, people were just starting to trickle in, all of them smiling at her.

"Come, eat!" she shouted to them. "I prepared this all by myself."

One of the men approaching her beamed. "It's hard work satisfying a goddess. Good morning." He took her hand and kissed it gently. Raziel felt her heart warm as she dragged a finger down his beard when he dropped her hand.

In the distance, a loud rumbling could be heard, and it perked Raziel up instantly.

"Shall we dance in the rain?" she exclaimed.

Numerous people eagerly agreed, and as she put her own plate together, her excitement started to creep in. Raziel loved the rain and felt like there was no other natural force that had the same power as a rainstorm. As they all finished their breakfast, the clouds began to open and pour down over the compound.

"Come! Let's go! Now!" she shouted at them.

Many people followed her out and spun around in the falling raindrops. Raziel held her arms out and tilted her head back, allowing herself to succumb to the sheer beauty of the storm. And almost as if it were queued, a bright bolt of lightning lit up the sky over them, causing Raziel to gawk at it.

"You see? The storm wants to dance, too! Keep going!" she bellowed, causing the other members of the group to increase their intensity.

The rain started to get heavier, challenging them to dare to stay outside. Once the thunder sounded like it was outside of the gates, Raziel finally ushered the group back inside, just in time for dinner. They all ran in and were met with plush towels to wrap around themselves. The rain outside looked like a water curtain outside the window;

they all watched in awe as it moved the trees outside the walls.

"Have you seen Troy?" one of the kitchen maids asked as she dropped some potatoes onto Raziel's plate during dinner.

Raziel faked a look of concern and replied, "I haven't seen him since yesterday."

"That's odd. He went to go talk to you. Are you saying he didn't even do that?"

Raziel shook her head. "Nope, I didn't see him at all." She made sure to force a look of concern as she looked around the room, pretending to look for him.

As the other people looked around the room also, and some ran into the kitchen, Raziel felt a pang of nervousness start to creep up in her stomach. There were murmurs floating through the crowd, and Raziel knew she needed to get on top of it.

She stood up and whistled. Everyone's heads turned to her, and she calmly said, "Perhaps Troy left. We hadn't been seeing eye-to-eye for some time, and maybe he thought it would be best for him to leave Nirvana. If that is truly the case, we will wish him nothing but the best for his future endeavors." The humans looked around at each other, and then back to Raziel with concern in their eyes. Raziel looked around and made eye contact with each of them. She could feel her eyes dilating as she said, "We wish Troy nothing but love and happiness outside of these walls."

In monotone voices, the entire room repeated, "We wish Troy nothing but love and happiness outside of these walls," as their pupils dilated twice as large as usual.

Raziel clapped her hands together and yelled, "Yes, exactly!"

The group started to shake their heads slightly before going back to their conversations.

As everyone settled back into their individual spots, Raziel sighed in relief. Now they could move on, Troy would become a distant memory, and no one would look for him until the foraging group came back. Raziel gripped the bridge of her nose. She had almost forgotten about the foraging group and knew they would look for Troy when they came back, or mention that they hadn't seen him in the city. But that was an issue for the future, and she didn't want to ruin the vibe that had taken over.

Raziel quickly wolfed down the rest of her dinner and rushed out into the rain, clasping a blanket over her, and ran toward her cabin. When she walked in, the blanket was thoroughly soaked, so she hung it over the garden fence. She glimpsed at the freshly dug-up rosebush and back up to the sky. She felt a sense of relief. The flowers would be well hydrated, and the compound wouldn't wonder about Troy.

But then she felt uneasy. It was unusually dark, and her senses were on full alert. She scanned the room and quietly said, "Natalia?"

Out of the darkest shadows, her sister stepped out into the limited light coming through the window. She scanned Raziel and raised her brow at her nakedness. Raziel grabbed a dry blanket that was slung over the small chair beside the door and wrapped it around herself.

"Sister, what are you doing here?"

Natalia looked at her nails to admire them and said, "Did you not get my message?"

"Your… message?"

She looked around, and Natalia sneered. "I killed your garden for the better part of a day, Sister. Do you not check your garden daily?"

Raziel rolled her eyes. "That was you?"

Natalia slowly clapped. "Very good, Sister. Well done, you solved the mystery."

Raziel scrunched her face. "You don't need to be like that."

Natalia dramatically sat down on the bed, and she said, "You know what's coming up, don't you?"

Raziel nodded. "Yes, I can feel her hunger."

"We need to make sure that it doesn't get as bad as last time. I don't think her kingdom could recuperate like it did before. It's already incredibly thinned out."

Raziel listened, cautiously asking, "Has Azazel built her chamber yet?"

Natalia shrugged. "I don't think so. Her festival is taking place, and they are due to choose the sacrifices in the next several days."

Raziel sighed. "But that is what triggers it."

"True, but if we stay ahead of it, perhaps she wouldn't want to build her chamber again."

Raziel looked at her skeptically. "It's Azazel. She will *always* have a want—a need for that death chamber."

Natalia scoffed. "What does it matter to you? They are humans, vermin that can reproduce effortlessly." She looked at Raziel. A wicked smile came over her face. "Sister, don't tell me you've fallen in love with one."

Raziel quickly looked up at Natalia, "No, of course not!"

Natalia laughed. "Right, I almost forgot that you're incapable of love. It's all mimicked." Her cackle filled every corner of the small cabin. "Sister, I must admit, it's been a while since I have laughed like that. The thought of you trying to fall in love will *never* cease to be funny to me."

As she started to laugh again, Raziel stood up, angry. "Natalia, you're on your own this time. I want to be left alone."

Natalia stopped laughing, stood up, and walked over to stand in front of Raziel. She placed her hand on Raziel's shoulder. "Sister, true love is true pain. I promise you that you're not missing anything. You're quite blessed that you can't feel true love. You'd never survive it."

Raziel shrugged her sister's hand off of her and quietly said, "You know nothing. I've seen humans fall in love and can feel the energy that it radiates. It's the only thing that matters." She could feel tears starting to fill her eyes, and she turned her face away.

But Natalia turned Raziel's head back to face her. "Sister, you know we need to do this together. I will keep an eye on Azazel, and when I return, you know it will be dire."

Raziel nodded, and when she looked back, Natalia was gone. She let a sigh out and sat down on the chair nearest to her. She hated how condescending Natalia was, and was always relieved when their interactions were over. Raziel thought of Azazel's kingdom and the people who lived there, knowing that some were about to sacrifice family members to appease her hunger. She felt sick.

She was angry that her sisters could feel love if they wanted to, but instead, they chose to treat their human charges as enslaved people and livestock. Regardless of how many times she brought up her concerns with them, they would brush them aside and tell her that she was crazy to want to live in peace with her humans.

The thought of Troy's withering body slowly crept its way back into her mind, and she felt sick. Was she *really* that much better than her sisters? She looked out the window in the direction of the rose garden, knowing how many bodies were buried underneath those bushes.

Raziel leaned back against the chair and let out a sigh. She *wasn't* better than her sisters, no matter how much she tried to convince herself that she was; the only difference was that she didn't give in to her divine primal needs unless she was angry enough to do so.

She shook her head, frustrated. Whenever Natalia came

around, she always ended up questioning herself and what she was doing, even though her sisters literally consumed humans like they needed them in order to breathe. She stood up and walked over to the closet, pulling out a simple pink dress. She slipped it over her head and left the cabin and her insecurities behind.

The further Raziel walked from the cabin, the more at peace she felt, and before she walked into the maternity cabin, she took a deep breath and replaced her furrowed brow with a forced smile. She was ready for baby cuddles. But when she walked into the cabin, she was shocked to see a man standing there, holding the baby. Raziel looked from Lily to him, and realized that he was one of the builders in the community, Brian.

He turned around and drew a wide grin on his face. "She's beautiful, isn't she?" Then he looked back to the sleeping Oriana in his arms. Lily watched the scene, and Raziel could feel the intense emotions radiating from her.

Raziel blurted out, "You're the father?"

Brian and Lily both nodded, and Raziel asked, "With the events that go on around here, how can you be sure?"

Brian and Lily looked at each other nervously, then Lily responded. "We have never been intimate with other people."

Raziel felt her rage starting to bubble from the deepest parts of her body. "There are *no* monogamous relationships in Nirvana!"

Lily held her hand out. "We weren't going to say anything, and we aren't monogamous. We've… just never been intimate, or felt the need to be intimate, with anyone else."

Raziel glared at the two of them, and she seethed. "All three of you are leaving in the morning."

Lily gasped. "You can't be serious! You expect me to trek through the dense forest with a newborn baby?!"

Raziel shrugged and carelessly said, "Sounds like you have everything you need within each other. You no longer need Nirvana. Get out!" And she turned to leave the cabin as quickly as she could.

As Raziel stood outside the door, she felt a strange feeling when her eyes started to overflow with tears filled with betrayal. She had given them *everything* that they could possibly ever want in life; why would they bring *monogamy* into the compound?

She walked away from the cabin, her entire head buzzing with everything that had just transpired. Between Natalia showing up and finding out that members of her commune were keeping themselves from other people, Raziel felt like she was losing control.

Lily's first day at Nirvana ran through Raziel's mind. She remembered how shy the young girl was, and how she used to jump to be the first one to do any task that needed to be done. For a small-framed woman, she was incredibly strong and resilient.

She shook her head and buckled down on her decision. The first rule every newcomer was told was that there was absolutely no monogamy. This was a free-loving community, and everyone was to engage with everyone else. Raziel saw hundreds of fireflies floating out of the forest, and they seemed to light a path for her. It helped her calm herself down by the time she reached her cabin. She was more than ready to sleep all night.

When she reached the front door, she paused before grabbing the doorknob. Half expecting her sister to be waiting for her on the other side, she cautiously opened the door and peeked around it. When she saw that she was alone, Raziel walked inside, slammed the door shut, and threw herself onto the bed. She closed her eyes and summoned sleep to come to her.

Natalia's words floated through her head; Raziel *had* felt like Azazel's reset was approaching. She felt the disturbance deep inside of her, and whenever the hunger was taking over, things in Nirvana became chaotic. Regardless of how many times Natalia and Raziel had tried, they couldn't figure out how Azazel's needs affected their domains. When Azazel was sleeping and was forced to stay still, things flourished, and Raziel thrived.

In her sleep, Raziel fell into a time when Nirvana was lush and full of life and love. Everyone was carefree, and the world seemed light and easy. The reset ritual came next, Natalia and Raziel holding hands, whispering an incantation in a language only angels could understand, and watched as Azazel glowed brighter than a star being birthed. And when the glow subsided, both Natalia and Raziel felt invigorated, as if they had just been touched by the hand of the Creator.

Images of past humans who had been thrown into the rose garden pit started to float around through the images of the reset, asking why they weren't worthy of life outside of Nirvana. Raziel pushed them aside, trying to get back to her good feeling. The faces started to fade and were replaced with a dark shadowy figure. Raziel could barely make out the face in the darkness, but she felt a fluttery feeling in her stomach. She felt safe and truly happy, something she had never really felt before.

When Raziel opened her eyes and saw that she had slept through the entire night, she frowned; she was curious about the figure who wouldn't leave her dreams. Whenever she saw those types of images in her dreams, it was usually an indication of something else to come. Raziel wouldn't know until it was happening, but it was something that she would start to look forward to. Perhaps it was an indication that new people would be called to find themselves in Nirvana, and whatever it was, Raziel was excited at the new prospect.

When she stepped out of the cabin, she was overtaken by the scent of the rose bushes. Raziel closed her eyes and took a deep breath; the scent could calm her down even on the most hectic days. They were her most prized possessions, and there were some that could be traced all the way back to the beginning of Nirvana, still producing the most beautiful blooms she had ever seen.

She walked slowly in the direction of the dining hall. She wasn't even halfway across the field when Sarah came running toward her, a look of horror on her face when she saw Raziel. When she got close enough, she desperately asked, "Lily, Brian, and Oriana left Nirvana this morning; why?"

Raziel looked at her, and she calmly asked, "What is rule number one here, Sarah?"

Sarah's face scrunched up in confusion. "But Lily and Brian weren't in a monogamous relationship, Raziel."

Raziel grabbed Sarah's arm and aggressively pulled her close as she hissed, "They admitted to only being intimate and enjoying each other. No one else was welcome. What does that sound like to you?"

Sarah's eyes started to water. "Why would you let them leave? They won't make it out of the forest alive!"

Raziel tilted her head and replied, "You make it sound like it's my problem when I was explicitly clear about the rules to living in Nirvana. If you don't agree, you're more than welcome to go after them. They may need an extra set of hands."

Raziel let Sarah's arm go, causing Sarah to slowly back away from her. "You're going to regret it," she spat as she pointed at Raziel before running away from her.

The fallen angel watched Sarah run away from her and felt that her morning was already ruined. "I just want one full day of peace and quiet. Why is that so hard?" No one was around to answer her, and she knew she would never get a sign, but she needed to ask it out loud.

Once she calmed herself down, Raziel decided that she no longer wanted to eat or see anyone, so she turned around and started walking toward the new garden location. Working in the soil always made her feel better, and she would be able to ground herself properly.

When she approached the garden, she was relieved to see that she was the only one there, and she grabbed one of the empty baskets, slowly filling it with fresh tomatoes. Raziel had harvested half of the first part of the garden before she stopped, hearing people approaching.

She turned around and called out, "I'm going to handle the garden today. Perhaps there are other jobs that need to be done. Maybe later, you can start pickling some of this harvest." She forced a smile toward them, but none of them returned it; they simply bowed and backed away from the garden.

Raziel continued to fill four more baskets with tomatoes. When she ran out of baskets, she started stacking them beside the garden, intending to get sacks to carry them into the kitchen. Before she knew it, the sun was over top of her, and she was covered in soil. Raziel fell to her knees and started to cry over Lily, Brian, and Oriana, and over the responsibility that she carried for Azazel. For the first time in a very long time, she fully allowed herself to succumb to her sadness. She collapsed onto the ground, tears watering the grass around her face. She gripped the ground, digging her nails in, begging for relief from the overwhelming pressure that she was feeling.

When she felt like she could no longer cry, she raised her head, and in the places where her tears had fallen, light pink flowers were starting to grow. Raziel looked at them, and when she picked one up, it died and fell apart in her fingers.

She had never seen anything like it, and she looked around her, wondering if Natalia was behind it.

But instead of seeing her sister, she felt a breeze caress her face and bees buzzing around the flowers. The negative feeling soon subsided, and Raziel stood up, ready to face her community. The tiny flowers withered and retreated back into the ground beneath her as she stood on her feet. Raziel stared at the spot for a few moments, trying to figure out what was happening, until she realized how quiet it was. She looked around and didn't see anyone in the clearing or anywhere near the cabins. Nervousness crept up into her stomach. She grabbed two baskets and started to walk toward the kitchen, unsure of what she would find when she reached it.

6

As Raziel approached the building, she was relieved to hear laughter inside. When she opened the door, the group stopped and looked at her. Raziel could tell that they were bracing themselves for some sort of outburst. Instead, she gently placed the baskets on the island in front of her and smirked at them all.

She took a deep breath and calmly said, "I have harvested the entire garden. I will need some help bringing them all in, but we also have a large task ahead of us, jarring and pickling after the ritual this weekend."

The kitchen staff exchanged looks. Sarah stepped forward to bring one of the baskets closer.

As she got close to Raziel, she quietly asked, "Are you okay? I'm here to listen if you need to talk, you know."

Raziel took Sarah's hand and responded, "That would be appreciated. Let's go sit by the water after lunch. I have so much weighing my heart down."

Sarah bowed. "Sure. Please come find me when you are ready."

Raziel nodded and backed out of the kitchen to retrieve the rest of the harvest, followed by several kitchen workers. They were all buzzing with excitement over the upcoming full moon and the abundance that it was already bringing to Nirvana.

If only her people truly knew how much influence Raziel had on the abundance and well-being of Nirvana, they would change the ritual into a ritual for her and allow her to feed off of the energy that they radiated willingly. Raziel felt her mouth water when she thought of the power that could have been hers if she were just selfish enough to convince her followers to do so.

She sighed quietly and looked back. "This ritual is going to be special; it's the blood moon." Raziel thought of past rituals for the blood moon and felt herself indulging in the anticipation as well. She always looked forward to the full moon. It was the one time she felt truly connected to Earth and the people around her; the energy that radiated from the group was unmatched.

As they reached the garden, Raziel handed each person a basket and started to pile some of the fresh vegetables and fruits on top of it, and sent them on their way. As she grabbed the last basket, the remaining harvest could wait until after they ate their lunch. The group was already ahead of Raziel, and she could hear the low chatter as they returned to the kitchen.

She placed the basket outside and called in, "I'll be taking my lunch at the maternity cabin. Could someone bring me a plate?"

Someone shouted back that they would, and Raziel left the kitchen, her sadness increasing the closer she got to her destination. When she reached the cabin, she opened it and was surprised to see how clean everything was. Lily cared enough to ensure that there wasn't a trace of her before she left, and even made sure to fold up the bedsheets and other blankets that were dropped off for her.

Raziel felt a pit in her stomach, wondering if she had indeed crossed a line by banishing them. She fell to the ground and was bombarded with the memory of welcoming Oriana into the world, how scared Lily was, and the way she looked to Raziel to be her source of comfort. She wiped a tear from her eye as she remembered the first time she saw Oriana and how absolutely perfect she was.

When she looked through the window and saw birds flying across the branches, she thought that perhaps the one way she would be able to feel true love like Lily and Brian was if she allowed monogamy into the compound. Raziel let her head fall back as she closed her eyes; knowing that she wouldn't be having these thoughts if it weren't for a good reason, she stood up and decided that she needed to go find them. She heard a soft knock at the door and got up to answer it. Sarah was standing on the other side of the door with a tray of food.

Raziel looked at her, and in a broken voice, she said, "I need to find Lily."

Sarah bowed and handed her the tray. "I know. We will go find them after you eat." She stepped into the cabin.

Raziel stepped aside so Sarah could fully enter the cabin. Once she was in, she shut the door with a free hand and brought the tray over to the small table off to the side of the large bed. Sitting down and starting to pick at the fruit,

Sarah sucked air through her teeth. "Raziel, can I speak candidly?"

"Unburden your mind, Sarah, then I'll do the same."

Sarah took a deep breath before saying, "Brian and Lily aren't the only ones who have chosen to exhibit monogamy in Nirvana. They were just the only ones to have been caught." She watched Raziel's face as she continued, "We all love you, Raziel; whether you believe it or not, we are all incredibly devoted to you and your ideas. We are more than dedicated to enforcing the reality that you want to bring. Monogamy doesn't change any of that. We just want to be able to choose."

"Are there more people who are leaning toward this path?"

"Our feelings don't change for you, and we will do everything in our power to ensure that you never feel a lack of our love."

Raziel let out a long sigh. "I agree, Nirvana is not above change, and maybe it's time that we move forward and embrace free love and the choices that it brings. We will go search for them today, and when we return, we will have a community meeting and take a vote. I want everyone to have their say. I won't fight it, and I will embrace everyone and their choices with open arms."

Sarah stared at Raziel in disbelief; she whispered, "Really?"

"Get a group together. I will meet you at the gates shortly."

Sarah bowed and stood up to rush out of the cabin. Raziel felt as if a weight had been lifted, hoping that it would get rid of the negative fog that had been hovering around as of late. She sighed and pushed the half-eaten meal away from her. When she had first started Nirvana, she made it clear that everyone was to enjoy each other; never did she think that people would eventually want to couple up and move away from that lifestyle.

She felt a pang of jealousy start to boil deep inside of her. She wanted to feel, truly feel, what the humans felt when they were falling in love with each other, and she wanted it for herself. Raziel was almost brought to tears, knowing that regardless of how hard she tried, she could never *truly* feel love. She sat there for a few moments as countless thoughts ran through her mind, memories of celebrations that she took part in, and the delicious entanglements that Nirvana took part in; she hoped that more people would opt to stay in an open lifestyle.

Standing up, Raziel felt that it was time to search for her beloved Lily and Oriana. She hadn't gotten to know Brian on a more personal level, but the work he did around Nirvana was impeccable, and he seemed incredibly genuine, from what she did know. When she stepped outside, the sun seemed to be shining brighter than before, and even the grass looked greener the longer she stared at it.

When she approached the gates, she was happy to see a group of people waiting for her. When they saw her approaching, they all waved and smiled widely at her. Raziel knew that when they found Lily, she would have an incredible amount of apologizing to do and hoped that Lily would find it in her heart to forgive her.

They opened the gates and walked into the dense rainforest on the beaten path leading out to the world. It had been decades since Raziel walked out of Nirvana, and the beauty the forest held made her regret it.

Monkeys were swinging through the trees above them as colorful birds sung their songs. Raziel took a deep breath in and was comforted by the thick, warm air; it felt like a hug. The group was quiet until they came to a fork in the path. Sarah looked back at Raziel, and she suggested that the group split up; one led into the city, and the other led to a water source deeper within the forest.

The group quickly split, and Raziel took half of them toward the water. As they got closer, they could hear the bugs buzzing and frogs croaking. When they reached the large waterfall, they gasped at the beauty it held; the water was ice blue and surrounded by lush, bright green fauna. Raziel looked around and basked in the beauty, suddenly grateful for the opportunity to come back out into the forest. The others in the group all wanted to cool off, so they all decided to hop into the waterfall's basin. Excited squeals erupted from the group as they realized how cold the water was, but once they adjusted, they shouted gratitude to the Universe for the blessing bestowed upon them.

After some time, the other search party found them, and when Raziel saw Sarah's face, she knew something was wrong. She lifted herself out of the water and ran over to the group, all of their faces white, and half of them looking like they were in shock.

Raziel looked at all of them and asked, "What happened? Did you find them?"

Sarah started sobbing and shook her head. "We found them, but…" She trailed off, and Raziel urged her to continue. Sarah barely got out, "They didn't make it."

Raziel shook her head and looked around at the group. "No, that can't be. They left during the day. They stayed on the path, right?"

One of the men, Kody, came forward, and he quietly said, "It looks like something attacked them. They didn't get close to the city; it was a brutal scene. We dug holes for them; that's why it took us so long to get back here."

Raziel grasped her face and shook her head in disbelief.

Sarah watched her leader, and she whispered, "See what

happens when you act on your impulses; we are the ones who pay for it!"

Raziel shook her head. "We will honor them tonight with a funeral pyre."

The group looked at each other again.

Sarah asked in an angry voice, "You think that will suffice?! Three people are *dead* because of your stupid rules. Take the vote now. Get everyone's opinions on what we talked about in the maternity cabin. Now!"

Raziel looked down at the ground; she quietly said, "Fine."

She motioned for the group to follow her to the waterfall, where the other half of the group was watching, curious as to what happened. When Raziel told them, they cried out, their sorrow deafening.

Raziel cleared her throat, and she loudly said, "Some rules are going to be changed. The first one is that if you want to be with one person only, you're free to. There are no rules when it comes to intimate relationships." This caused the group to gasp in surprise. Raziel continued, "The second new rule is that if someone is going to be banished, we are going to take a vote as a whole to see if anyone can come up with reasons as to why they should stay, and if they are deemed worthy reasons, they will be allowed to stay."

She looked at Sarah, who nodded in approval, and her arms were crossed over her body. When she looked up at Raziel, her eyes were filled with tears. Raziel felt guilty and now understood the weight of her actions. She knew that she may never know true human love, but she was finally starting to understand true human pain and loss. She didn't like it, and she wanted to avoid ever feeling it again.

The entire group silently made their way back to Nirvana, none of them in the mood to continue playing in the water.

The air was heavy with sorrow, and Raziel wished she could take all of the pain away. She wasn't sure how she was going to tell the foragers what happened when they returned, just to go through the mourning process all over again.

As they walked through the gates, none of them spoke to Raziel, and she concluded that she would be building the funeral pyre herself. She was okay with it; she wanted to and wanted to put enough care into it so that Lily, Brian, and sweet Oriana felt how sorry she was wherever they were beyond the veil. While the group split off to break the news to the other members of the commune, Raziel went to a secluded shed in the back of the property that contained wood left over from other construction projects.

She single-handedly built a giant pyramid and found sweet grass to put inside of it. She then went to her rose garden and cut the majority of the flowers from the countless bushes, and created a garland long enough to wrap around the entire structure. When she was finished constructing the pyre, she took a step back and was pleased with her work. Raziel was sad that she had let her jealousy and anger make such impulsive decisions. While she constructed the pyre, she thought of the many years she shared with Lily and put the emotion that she knew as love into every bit of it.

She didn't hear the rest of the community approaching her as she was lost in her memories. Sarah gently placed her hand on Raziel's shoulder. She quietly said, "It's beautiful. Lily would have loved it. You took a step in the right direction today, and I'm proud of you for attempting to right your wrongs. You have to remember that we are a bit more fragile than you."

Raziel nodded, knowing she was right. In the grand scheme of things, human lives were always so delicate. She knew that this group of people was her responsibility, her children, and she needed to act accordingly. She looked around at her community as they wrapped their arms around each other, sobbing and calling Lily, Brian, and Oriana's names out.

The fire began to creep up the pyre, engulfing the entire structure in flames. The commune was quiet as they all watched the fire take over the pyramid, smoke billowing up to the blanket of stars watching them mourn their loss. Once the structure had dulled down and crumbled to ashes, the silence that followed was something that Raziel had never experienced before. While there were countless deaths at Nirvana, she had never felt the weight of loss like this. She looked around the group and made sure to take in each of their emotions; Raziel wanted to carry the weight for everyone since these deaths were on her hands.

It wasn't long before someone in the crowd started to sing a hauntingly beautiful song. The group began to hum, and Raziel simply listened, taking in their pain and praying that the small family hadn't suffered for long. Once the singer finished, they all began to slowly disperse from the pyre until it was only Sarah and Raziel left, watching the coals glow. Raziel looked at her, and even in the dull light, she could see how hard Sarah had been crying. She held her breath as she walked the short distance to stand beside her; Raziel grabbed her hand and squeezed it.

Sarah pulled her hand away from Raziel and turned to her. The look on Sarah's face was replaced by anger, and she hissed, "This is all your fault."

She took a step closer to Raziel, causing her leader to step back in surprise and respond, "I know it is, Sarah. I take full responsibility. I feel like I have made that abundantly clear."

Sarah shook her head. "It's not enough."

Raziel looked at her in shock. "What would you like me to do about it?"

Sarah shrugged. "That's your job. Figure it out, Great Leader. Building the funeral pyre wasn't the solution, and you have a lot of hurt to heal."

She quickly turned around and headed toward the cabins for the night, leaving Raziel to stew in her emotions and thoughts.

7

Raziel waited until the fire had completely died down before she turned to go back to her own cabin. It was pitch black as she walked across the clearing, the dew on the grass soaking the bottom of her skirt and feet. By the time she reached her cabin, her skirt was thoroughly soaked, and she had started to develop a chill. She looked up at the moon, and while it wasn't completely full, she figured it would be a perfect night to take a moon bath and shed off some of the guilt that she felt.

Raziel walked through her cabin to the back, where there was a small deck with a large clawfoot bathtub surrounded by candle-filled lanterns. She started to fill the large tub from the water reservoir beside it and pulled a medium-sized fire bowl from under the tub to start the healing process as she lit it and pushed it back underneath the tub. Once the tub was filled with water and beginning to warm, Raziel took a thin piece of wood, gathered some of the fire, and walked around the deck to light all of the candles, casting a soft glow around the deck.

As she undressed, she let her head fall back and felt admiration for the location of her cabin. The opening in the trees allowed her to have a full view of the moon above her, allowing the moonlight to charge her bath and heal her with its magic.

When she placed her hand into the water, she was content to find that the water was as hot as she wanted. She pulled the firepit from under the tub and allowed it to brighten the glow around her. Raziel stepped into the tub and lowered herself into it. Sighing in pleasure, she closed her eyes and placed her arms on either side of the tub.

After a few moments, she opened her eyes again and into the darkness beyond the lanterns. "I attract all of the pain my people feel. I embrace it and release it into the Universe to heal." Raziel waited, challenging the darkness, and when she didn't feel anything come rushing to her, she started to lean back.

All of a sudden, as if she were electrocuted by lightning, her back arched, and all of the pain, frustration, and sorrow rushed into Raziel's body. She started to shake as if it were going to completely consume her until she shot her head back, and a fast stream of black smoke poured out of her mouth and spiraled up to the sky.

Once she felt completely empty, her body collapsed back into the water. Raziel opened her eyes and looked around as if something were to come out of the woods. When nothing jumped, she relaxed her body and sighed. Tomorrow was going to be a new day at Nirvana, and with the negativity that everyone was carrying officially gone, Raziel knew they could genuinely heal. In addition, it was the day that the foragers were supposed to be returning, and they would be spending the day preparing for the ritual the following night.

Raziel was exhausted, but she felt herself smirk. The ritual always brought everyone together, and they rode the waves of love and happiness for weeks afterward. Raziel looked forward to having everyone be happy and together again.

She waited until the water had cooled entirely before she got out of the tub, pulling the plug and allowing the water to run freely. Raziel felt as if she had been renewed, and that the horrible events were draining out of the tub with it. She blew out the candles and snuffed the small fire out. When she went back into the cabin, she felt as if she had walked into a wall of exhaustion. After she dried herself off and rubbed lotion all over her body, she crawled into her bed, grateful that she was able to take her family's pain away, hopeful that they would be able to move past it the next day. When Raziel finally fell asleep, she fell into a deep sleep, dark, with no dreams or nightmares.

When she woke up the following morning, she felt like she had slept for hundreds of years. Completely rejuvenated, she jumped out of bed and quickly got dressed. She then walked out the front door and was taken aback by how bright the sun was.

It felt like a new day at Nirvana, and even the energy outside of her own cabin was light-hearted and felt nothing short of amazing. While she remembered the night before and knew what had happened, Raziel wasn't sure how the people would react when they saw her.

As she walked to get her breakfast, the people she passed offered smiles and morning greetings. Raziel was cautious, but she was thrilled to see that people were in higher spirits. Before she entered the kitchen, Raziel took a deep breath, bracing herself. When she opened the door, the entire kitchen was abuzz with excitement. The chef was cooking up chocolate chip pancakes, and Raziel saw a mountain of strawberries waiting to be devoured. She picked up a fat berry and popped it into her mouth. The juice was sweet, and it was the most perfect strawberry she had ever tasted.

The chef looked at her and sweetly asked, "Would you like me to prepare you a plate?"

Raziel shook her head. "No, I can wait. I just wanted to see how everyone was feeling."

Suddenly, Sarah came rushing in from the dining room and had a large grin on her face. "Raziel! Good morning!" She beamed.

Good, it's working. "Good morning, Sarah. How are you?"

Her eyes twinkled as she replied. "Just awesome! The sun is beautiful, *and* we have a full moon tonight. There is nothing better!"

Raziel chuckled in relief; perhaps her negativity release worked better than she'd intended. She felt her heart swell with ease and happiness. Her community was going to return to normal, and the mourning period was short and sweet.

The chef interrupted her thoughts by announcing, "Breakfast is ready!"

Raziel smirked and ran to the dining room, ready to indulge in one of her favorite breakfasts.

Everyone talked amongst themselves, and Raziel did her rounds to each table before taking a seat. The other pregnant women were ecstatic to see her, and she placed her hands on each of their bellies, silently begging the babies to kick, to acknowledge her. The mothers weren't as far along as Lily was, but she felt like they would be here within the next three full moons.

As she held the last mother's belly, the unborn baby kicked hard. Raziel looked up at the mom "He's a feisty one."

The mother grasped her belly. "He?"

Raziel nodded. "I'm getting very strong male energy from him."

The mother started to cry tears of joy and grasped Raziel's hands in gratitude. Raziel continued to her table and started to eat her breakfast. She felt complete and hopeful as if it were the first several days of Nirvana, and it oozed promise. When she finished her meal, she put the empty dishes in the bins, and when she walked out of the dining room, the group was waiting for her outside.

Raziel took them all in and opened her arms as she declared, "Let's get the firepit set up and tables brought out. The amethyst cathedrals need to be dragged up from the shed as well, while candles and fairy lights need to be placed in their normal spots."

Several people left the group with their tasks while others waited. Raziel looked at them and said, "Let's get enough flowers together to make a path from the gates to the firepit. I want the foragers to feel the immense love we have for them when they return. There are several species that can be found in the forest. Be careful; take weapons with you and the large baskets. Only the most beautiful blooms must be picked and brought back."

The other members of the group left her and headed toward the gates. Raziel was ready for her only task of the day. It was up to her to harness energy from the moon and disperse it across Nirvana; it helped to keep the protective barrier strong for Nirvana to stay the way it was.

Raziel walked down to the water source, and when she reached the riverbank, she didn't stop. She stepped over the surface of the water, and when she reached the middle of the large lake and sat down, she crossed her legs and placed both of her palms on the surface of the water and closed her eyes. She could still feel the moon's energy buzzing around her, and she focused on it, pulling it into her and feeling it shoot out of her fingers and into the water, radiating from her. She felt the entire place buzz with the energy, and she focused on strengthening Nirvana from the core, from *her* core.

Raziel sat on the water's surface for hours until she heard her name being called. She turned her head to see Sarah running and pointing to the gates. The foragers had returned. Raziel stood up and walked back to land. As her foot touched the bank, she started to run across the clearing. She saw countless totes and bags being brought through the gates and more people returning, hugging each other.

When Ramona came through the gates and saw Raziel, they sprinted toward each other. Raziel pulled her into a long hug, gripping the back of her head as she whispered, "I've missed you. There is much to talk about."

Ramona pulled back from her and nodded. "There is."

As she looked back to the gates, the most beautiful man Raziel had ever seen walked through. Ramona looked to Raziel, whose breath was taken entirely. The group welcomed him, and each person hugged him, welcoming him to the compound.

Raziel walked over to him, and it felt as if time had stopped. He smiled warmly at her, revealing perfectly straight white teeth; she looked him up and down. He had shoulder-length shaggy blonde hair, piercing blue eyes, a jawline that wouldn't stop, and broad shoulders. He extended his large hand toward her, and Raziel took it, surprised by how soft it was.

A small gasp escaped her lips, and she stumbled over her words as she said, "Welcome to Nirvana. I am Raziel."

He nodded and shook her hand slowly as he replied in a deep and seductive voice. "I am Angelus, and I am looking for enlightenment."

Raziel placed her other hand on his arm, taken back by how muscular he felt. "You are in the right place, Angelus."

They stared at each other for some time until someone interrupted them by screaming, "You guys got the pink pitaya? Finally!"

Raziel pulled her hands from him and cleared her throat as she roared, "Can someone please show our newest initiate to the men's cabins, please?"

Several men stepped forward, clapping him on the back. As he walked away from the crowd, he looked back and smiled when he saw Raziel watching him leave. Ramona grabbed Raziel's arm and excitedly asked, "Did I do good?"

Raziel stared at her. "Where did he come from?"

Ramona giggled. "He approached us, but I haven't seen him act like that the entire time we were in the city."

Raziel tilted her head. "I'm intrigued."

Ramona laughed and replied, "I bet you are! He didn't seem to take an interest in any of us, either."

Raziel couldn't help but smile, for real this time. While she knew that she had some sort of an effect on men, it never ceased to amaze her how flirty they could get the first time in her presence.

Ramona coughed and asked, "What is it we need to discuss?"

Raziel took her hand and led her into the garden. She sat down and pulled Ramona down with her. Ramona looked around, and Raziel went on to tell her everything that had happened while they were gone. Ramona broke down in tears and screamed Lily's name; Raziel hugged her tight and placed her palms on the back of Ramona's head. She felt her palm start to tingle as she pulled the sorrow from Ramona's body, dulling her sobs to whimpers, and then finally, nothing. She pulled back from Raziel and wiped her nose.

"Lily is better off. This world is declining, and at least, she is at peace, and she knew true love before she passed."

Raziel nodded, even though the mention of *true love* made her feel like she had been impaled.

Raziel grabbed her hands as she whispered, "I know it's tough, but I promise it will stop hurting."

Ramona bowed. "I trust you. I already feel so much better."

They stared at each other, and Raziel radiated the love she could into Ramona, trying to fix her broken heart. Raziel then pulled back and asked, "What else can you tell me about our newest member?"

Ramona's eyes went wide as a wicked grin crept over her face. "Oh, my goodness, Raziel, wait until you see his body. His voice sounds *otherworldly*, and he seems incredibly hardworking. We barely had to explain things to him, and he was always quick to help us with whatever we needed."

Raziel listened closely, her excitement growing as Ramona spoke higher and higher of him. If he was highly recommended by one of her most favorite people, Raziel knew that he had *some* substance to him and was thrilled that he wanted to be a part of the community.

They stood up, and Raziel kissed Ramona on the cheek before she said, "Thank you. Thank you also for not dying out there."

Ramona blushed slightly, and they both walked to the kitchen to go over what had been brought back to Nirvana. As they entered, they could barely get through the door. Boxes of dry ingredients and supplies took up so much space, and people had begun to start jarring the garden harvest, the smell of cooking vegetables filling the air.

Watching everyone work toward a life of self-sufficiency

always brought Raziel so much pride in herself. She knew that while the outside world would suffer shortages eventually, the family within Nirvana's walls would always have full bellies and remain safe. Raziel stayed in the kitchen and helped the jarring and restocking process move quicker.

Under normal circumstances, she would show the newest members around, explain the rules, and learn more about them. But Angelus raised a feeling in Raziel that she had never experienced before; she was nervous, excited, and felt like she was on fire… all at the same time.

8

Once everything was cleaned up, the staff started to prepare lunch in their newly stocked kitchen. When Raziel stepped out of the kitchen, she saw Angelus and several other men constructing a small building; she looked at the group curiously and walked over. None of them acknowledged her until she cleared her throat loudly. They all stopped and looked at her.

One of the best carpenters in the compound, Tyler, stepped forward, and he said, "We are building a stargazing gazebo. We thought it would be the perfect addition to our ritual for tonight."

Raziel nodded, and indeed, it was already an incredibly

beautiful structure. She looked around the crowd and asked, "Who's idea was it?"

Angelus stepped forward, and he looked into her eyes directly. Raziel's breath caught in her throat. He ran his hands through his hair and said, "I wanted to showcase my talents. I heard you enjoy looking at the stars, and this was the best thing I could think of to honor you for allowing me to become part of the community." His expression changed as he jokingly scolded, "You weren't supposed to see it until it was finished; off you go."

Raziel was taken aback by his command, and while she would typically object, she nodded and replied, "I look forward to seeing it complete."

She wasn't sure what just happened, but she didn't want to give Angelus a wrong impression. Instead, Raziel walked around the compound to see how other aspects were going for the ritual. She was pleased to see that the lights were hung up and candles were spread out, while flowers were starting to take over the clearing. Raziel felt a sense of ease and allowed herself to begin to relax.

Walking around the compound, she suddenly heard the sound of a loud cowbell. She wasn't sure what was causing it but walked toward the ringing. When she found the cook signaling that it was time for lunch, Raziel smirked. It was smarter than word of mouth, and it was clearly working as people started to flock from all directions to the sound. Raziel hung back and allowed everyone else to flood into the dining room for their meal. She felt like she was witnessing a change that she didn't even know was needed. Something definitely had clicked into place.

Raziel scanned the room when she went inside and saw that Angelus was nowhere to be found. She waited for a few moments, but when everyone had begun to eat, he still didn't appear.

She walked down to where the new gazebo was with two full plates and found Angelus hammering nails on top of the roof; his shirt was off, and he was glistening with sweat under the sun. Raziel couldn't take her eyes off of him. It looked like he had been chiseled from stone. He was perfect.

She felt a fluttering feeling in her stomach, and when she got close enough, he yelled, "I was wondering when you'd show up!"

Raziel smirked. "Well, I figured you could use something to eat from all of the hard work."

Angelus put his hammer down and climbed down from the structure. He smiled and took a plate from her. "I also heard you're incredibly involved. I knew it was only a matter of time." He smiled at her and had a mischievous twinkle in his eye.

Raziel put on a fake look of annoyance. "You're talking about me behind my back?"

Angelus quickly responded, "I just wanted to know how to please you, so I asked questions." As he took a bite of fruit and looked up at her, Raziel could feel her cheeks start to flush. She was trying to fight the feeling that was coming up inside of her.

"How did you hear about Nirvana?"

Angelus sat down on the grass and patted the area across from him. Raziel sat down, and he began, "I come from a very small town. There were always whispers of a free-loving commune hidden in the middle of the rainforest, passed down through generations. Many places tried to replicate this." He motioned around him. "But I knew it wasn't the real thing. My parents tried to raise me in one of the copycat societies when I was young, but the rules became so severe over time that I ran away when I was fifteen."

Angelus looked down, and Raziel could feel that he was still upset about it. She quietly asked, "Are they still there?"

He shook his head. "They helped me escape, and I'm sure they were killed afterward as traitors. That was how they evolved over time. The leader became cruel and bloodthirsty. He demanded pure devotion and had a no-questions-asked regime."

Raziel listened to him, intrigued that people had tried to copy her; she had no idea that other communes had popped up. She was pleased that people wanted to embrace free love, but it needed to be peaceful; apparently, humans didn't understand that concept.

She looked at Angelus and asked, "How long have you been looking for Nirvana?"

He smiled. "My entire life."

"I'm glad you're here; we're all glad you're here. You're home, and you're welcome to stay for as long as you need to."

Angelus bowed, and a cloud seemed to cast over his face as he asked, "What kind of rules do you have here?"

Raziel put her plate to the side, and she answered, "While free love is encouraged, if monogamy is more your path, you're free to follow it. We all help raise any children who are born; we care for each other and work toward a better version of humanity as a collective."

Angelus listened and was focused on Raziel's face. He took everything in, and then looked around before. "I feel like I fit in here, like I was always meant to be here."

Raziel grabbed his hand. "I agree wholeheartedly."

They stared at each other for some time, and Raziel felt like Angelus was staring directly into her soul. Her breath caught in her throat, and she pulled her hand away.

Angelus quietly asked, "Did you feel that?"

Raziel quickly stood up. "I, uh, need to go check on the other members. Enjoy your lunch. Everyone will be back to help you shortly."

Angelus stood up as well. "Please don't leave just yet."

Raziel shook her head and replied, "I need to do my rounds. I will see you later." The look on Angelus' face broke her heart, but she needed to get away from what she was feeling. It was new, and she didn't know how to cope with it. "I will find you later."

He nodded and watched her quickly walk away.

Once Raziel was far enough, she realized that she had been holding her breath. She sighed and looked around her. She saw that Angelus was back on top of the gazebo, so she focused her attention back in front of her. Numerous people were starting to file out of the dining room and going off in their opposite directions to continue preparing for the ritual.

Ramona appeared through the crowd, and when she saw Raziel, her face lit up. Raziel saw her eyes shift behind her, and when she nodded, Ramona smiled even wider. They met halfway through the clearing when Raziel said, "We need to talk."

Ramona bowed and followed Raziel to her cabin. Once they were inside and the door was closed, Raziel whipped around to face Ramona. "Where did you find Angelus?"

Ramona's eyebrows furrowed, and she said, "He was in the city."

"*Where* in the city?" She had an urgency in her voice that Ramona had never heard before.

Ramona's face held a look of concern as she said, "He approached us. He seemed to just know that we weren't from the city, and he asked if we knew where he could find Nirvana; he was looking for inner peace and a sense of belonging."

Raziel was silent as she let the information settle. She started to pace around the cabin, and then she stopped. "Something is... magnetic about him; something is pulling me toward him on a divine level. I can't explain it."

Ramona smiled. "Could it be that you're experiencing love at first sight?"

Raziel shook her head. "Impossible. Utterly impossible!"

Ramona chuckled. "Many things have proven to be possible since I've been here. Lean into it, Raziel. It's okay. It'll do you some good to experience new things."

Raziel got a bit frustrated; humans would *never* understand what she was feeling. It wasn't like the type of love they were used to or could even comprehend.

The last time she'd felt any kind of pull like the one she was experiencing, she was still in service to the Creator. It was with one of the archangels, and it was the only time in her existence where she had ever felt anything *close* to being in love. In Heaven, they didn't call it *love*. It was simply a feeling that pulled angels together and paired them for eternity. What she was feeling with Angelus, felt like the same kind of magnetism that she'd felt right before the fall.

Raziel sighed; she felt uncomfortable and wasn't sure how long she could go before she gave into the feeling. Ramona was studying her and seemed to read her thoughts before she said, "I know it's scary, especially if you've never felt anything like it before, but the attraction you're feeling is so normal, Raziel. It's okay!"

She reached for Raziel, who pulled her hand away from Ramona. "It's fine, Ramona. I don't think you truly understand what I'm conveying, but it's quite alright. I'll figure it out."

Ramona took that as a dismissal, and before she exited the cabin, she looked back and said, "Raziel, sometimes new things set off alarms in our heads because it's an opportunity to grow from our past self. Growth is uncomfortable, but it's entirely worth it for your gain in the long run."

Raziel watched her leave and weighed the words that were spoken to her. While she knew that Ramona had some truth behind them, she also knew that Ramona would never understand the divine spectrum and what feelings comprised of that. She wasn't sure if it was love or not, but she felt something when Angelus looked at her, touched her, and spoke to her.

Raziel went over to her bedside table and pulled out a small teapot and a heating plate. She waited for it to heat up, and she grabbed a large teacup from the shelf below her other supplies. As she poured the hot water over the tea, Raziel tried to calm her nerves; she hoped that the peppermint would do the rest as she let it cool for a few moments before taking the first sip. The tea warmed her from the inside out, and Raziel felt like she was able to think clearly again.

She needed to get Angelus' face out of her head and focus on the ritual. It required her *entire* focus. Suddenly, the shadows from the darkest corners of the cabin stretched over the cabin's floor. She squinted her eyes and sighed as she heard Natalia's voice.

"Sister, hello."

Raziel looked over her shoulder, and Natalia stepped forward from the shadows. She walked to the front of the cabin and turned around. Raziel watched her stroll through her home as if she owned it, trying not to let it bother her. She gripped the cup harder and tried to keep her emotions locked down.

Natalia looked around her and took Raziel in completely. A slight smirk came over her face as she asked, "Is he here?"

Raziel looked up in surprise. "I'm sorry?"

Natalia's face morphed into a large grin. "I felt the ground beneath me shudder with the arrival of a new divine being."

Raziel shook her head. "No, no one is here."

Natalia's face turned downward in disappointment. "Too bad, I was looking forward to a battle royale."

Raziel looked up at her, seeing that Natalia wasn't kidding. She quietly said, "I simply want peace. I don't want to fight."

Natalia nodded. "That's alright. I welcome it and will gladly take on the violence." She looked around and tried to see if she could see any of the community members through the windows. When she couldn't, she turned back to Raziel. "You're telling me you didn't feel anything?"

Raziel shook her head. "No, I didn't."

Natalia's face dropped into a slight pout. "That's too bad. It was powerful. I'm sorry you missed it."

Raziel smiled weakly. "If anything happens, I will be sure to reach out, and we can assess together."

"Oh, Sister, I'm sure I'll feel it before you even see anything. I'll be in touch," and Natalia slipped back into the shadows.

Once she felt like she was truly alone, Raziel started to sip her tea again, going over the information that she was just told. By the time she finished her tea, it had grown dark, and it was time for the ritual to begin. She grabbed a silver circlet and placed it on her head. She then took a deep breath and left the cabin.

When she stepped outside, her breath was taken away. The entire compound was radiating a soft glow from the delicate lights and candles. Raziel walked the path to the large firepit as others came from all directions to surround her. When she saw Angelus standing on the opposite side of the pit, she felt nervous by the intensity of the look that he was giving her.

Raziel broke eye contact with him and looked around at the rest of her family. She opened her arms and loudly exclaimed, "Family, welcome! We are blessed again with this full moon. Let us thank the Universe for our blessings and our newcomer, Angelus. Welcome home."

Angelus smiled and looked around as people clapped quietly and murmured amongst themselves, giving thanks. They all circled around the pit as Raziel lit the flame. It wasn't long before a large fire shot up between them all. They all joined hands and began to chant up to the sky in a language that Raziel had taught them.

None of them would ever know that it was actually an incantation that would transfer some of their energy to her, and as they sang it, Raziel felt stronger, better, and her beauty was radiant. Once they finished, they hugged each other, and the kitchen staff ran to get food to continue the celebration. The fire was roaring, and someone suggested that they bring out some of the moonshine in honor of the full moon.

Raziel grinned; it *had* been a while since they had taken part in moonshine and agreed that it was a special occasion. She didn't see who ran off to get some, but all of a sudden, glasses were being passed out as the kitchen staff came back with planks filled with meat, cheeses, and pieces of bread. Raziel felt her heart swell, knowing that the night was going to be a good one.

Angelus was suddenly beside her. In a low tone, he said, "That song was beautiful. I apologize for not knowing the words."

Raziel smirked. "You'll learn."

He bowed. "It didn't sound familiar. What language was it?"

This caused Raziel to look at him. "A lost language."

Angelus took a step toward her. "I have learned many ancient languages. That didn't sound like any dialect I have heard before."

"It's a mix of Tamil and Aramaic."

Angelus nodded. "I thought I picked up some ancient Egyptian as well."

"Very good, there was some influence."

Angelus smiled wide. "Can I get you a refreshment? Some food?"

Raziel nodded and watched as he crossed over to the platters, weaving through the crowd.

When he returned, he had two glasses and one plate. He shyly said, "I thought we could share. Would you like to go down by the water?"

Raziel looked around and saw Ramona staring at the interaction with a grin on her face. Raziel could hear Ramona's voice in her head. "Just go with it!" So, she bobbed her head, and then followed Angelus. She looked back to see the group celebrating and whopping with excitement around the fire.

9

As they got to the lake, the glow from the fire and the rest of the lights were a dull glow. The only other light sources were the full moon overhead and the thousands of fireflies coming out of the surrounding woods. It was idyllic and romantic.

"It's so beautiful here," Raziel whispered.

Angelus agreed. "It truly is the definition of Nirvana."

Raziel smiled to herself. It was what she had always wanted to achieve. She wasn't sure what had happened over the last few days, but it truly transcended anything that she had ever experienced on Earth. Angelus handed her the plate that he had brought, and she popped some grapes into her mouth. Raziel felt like it was the first time she was eating the sweet fruit. They tasted sweeter than anything she had experienced before.

They sat in silence for several minutes, the sound of frogs and other small creatures filling the air. Angelus cleared his throat and asked, "Did you feel what I felt earlier?"

Raziel started to cough, choking on the bread that she had just taken a bite of. Once she stopped, she looked at him and cautiously said, "I felt *something*. I don't know what, though."

He quietly said, "I was sent here for a reason, Raziel." She felt her heart drop as Natalia's words floated through her head. He continued, "I was drawn to you the second I saw you. I have been looking my entire life for someone to make me feel the way that you have."

Raziel looked at him, and in the faint light, she could see the outline of his features, and she could feel the seriousness of the moment. She had never been confronted in this sense, and while she felt uncomfortable, she felt that perhaps the Universe was rewarding her for her dedication.

She took a deep breath, and she replied, "I have never felt the way that you make me feel, especially given that it has only been a day. I shouldn't feel like this."

Angelus placed a gentle finger over her lips. "Love has no time frame. I will spend every second of my life proving myself to you, if that's what you need."

Raziel was touched by his dedication already, but the moment was interrupted by the sound of people loudly approaching. She could hear the drunk slurring and figured that they were coming to the lake to cool off.

She whispered, "Let's continue this later."

As they stood up, the group of people reached them, only to run past them to jump into the lake. Squeals from the cold water filled the night air, and Raziel smirked in amusement.

Angelus asked, "Are you going to jump in?"

Raziel replied, "No, I'm going to go back to the fire. I'm starting to get cold. If you want to, please join them."

Angelus pulled all his clothes off and jumped into the water as if the moon were his personal spotlight. It seemed to increase in intensity as he came up from the depths, and it highlighted his muscular body. Raziel felt herself staring too long and shook her head to snap out of it. She turned to go to the firepit, her head a chaotic mess from what Angelus had told her.

When she reached the fire, Ramona was waiting and patted the ground beside her. She was holding a glass in her hand, and when Raziel sat down, she snatched the glass from Ramona and took a deep gulp.

Ramona stared at her. "Good talk?"

Raziel shook her head. "I don't know how to feel right now."

Ramona nodded. "Infatuation will do that. It turns you upside down and makes you question everything."

Raziel listened as she looked at the flames. "I don't know what to do, Ramona. I have so much responsibility; I can't lose myself like this."

Ramona grabbed Raziel's arm. "I can understand that, but at some point, it's okay to do something for yourself. It's okay to be happy."

"I know you're right. I know it's okay, but I can't allow myself to feel these things. In case something happens, I don't know *what* would happen if I were to have my heart broken, or if I break *his* heart."

"I can't tell you what to feel or how to feel. I can only tell you that it's *okay* to feel." Ramona pulled Raziel in for a side hug. The two sat in silence, passing the glass between them until the liquid was gone. The fire was starting to die down.

Eventually, Ramona whispered, "I'm tired; are you going to stay up a bit longer?"

Raziel shook her head. "No, I am ready to rest."

The two of them stood and hugged each other before parting ways. As Raziel walked to her cabin, she heard silence coming from the lake, happy that people had found their way back to their cabins, and that the compound was dying down for the night. She felt energized and was satisfied with the success of the ritual.

When she opened her cabin door, she was relieved to see that it was empty. Raziel quickly changed into a simple nightgown and crawled into bed, not even bothering to turn any lights on in the process. Her head had barely touched the pillow when she fell asleep.

She was thrust into a dark room, naked, and she felt complete bliss. When she reached her hand out, it was grabbed by a stronger one. It was attached to a muscular arm, and she found Angelus in bed with her.

The two engaged in a passionate affair, engulfing each other with lust. Raziel could feel the strength in his touch. While it was also delicate and soft, it was unlike anything she had ever felt before, on and off Earth.

When she woke up, she found the bottom half of her face covered with saliva, followed by the morning sun around her. She looked around; it felt so real. She touched her lips. Angelus' kiss was soft, yet earnest, and left her wanting more.

She lied back down and closed her eyes, hoping to slip back into the dream. Instead, when she fell back to sleep, she was thrown back into a time when she and her sisters were trying to repair humanity. Natural disasters had killed so many, and the sisters were sent to help rebuild society and help further humanity under the Creator's orders. He wanted them to advance but not enough so that they would ever question Him or His will.

They had been on Earth for months by the time they'd gotten frustrated enough by the slow advancement. Fights broke out between the three angels, and they went back and forth between giving the humans more knowledge and going back to the Creator to ask him to intervene. Eventually, they chose to talk to the Creator, and it led to the fall. Each sister was given a burden that they had to carry to ensure that they would *never* know true happiness.

Years flashed before Raziel's eyes as she watched humans experience true love while she was left empty and wanting more. The images were then replaced by Azazel's blood-covered body and Natalia's lifeless corpse draped over her.

Raziel sat up abruptly and was covered in sweat. She looked down and realized that she was shaking violently. The good feeling that she had was replaced with fear. Her dreams were usually prophetic, and while the first part was promising, she didn't feel hopeful about the entire experience. Raziel wondered if she should contact Natalia to tell her what she saw but chose not to act on it. Instead, she slid out of bed and slowly got dressed before leaving the cabin. The energy in the small home felt strange, and she wanted to get away from it.

When she stepped outside, she could smell something delicious and decided to follow the aroma. Angelus had several people by the firepit, and they were cooking something over a small flame. As Raziel approached the group, she scanned the faces and saw that Ramona wasn't there but continued walking toward them. She looked over to the gazebo, noticing that half of the roof was done. While it wasn't finished, she was impressed with how beautiful it was turning out.

When Angelus saw her approaching, he said something to

his companions, and they all made room for her and greeted her warmly. She looked around and asked, "What smells so delicious?"

Angelus smiled. "We are making biscuits and gravy."

"You're a man of many talents."

Angelus smirked. "You have no idea."

He handed her a warm biscuit with a small bowl of gravy. She took it from him, and when she tried it, she was surprised by how delicious it was. While the kitchen staff never failed to supply a delightful meal, this was a different experience and was somehow elevated.

Angelus leaned over and quietly asked, "Did you sleep well last night?"

Raziel stared at him and replied, "I did. How was your first night here?"

He looked over his shoulder and scanned the group in front of them. He then leaned in closer and whispered, "I couldn't get you out of my head. The dreams I had would make the most experienced sinner blush."

Raziel's mouth dropped open, and she felt herself getting hot. "Perhaps we shouldn't discuss such things in front of an audience."

Angelus bowed. "I'd much rather show you."

Raziel looked at him, and she could feel herself getting angry. "I am not just here to please you. I don't know what your idea of free love and a free community is, but I think you need some education."

"I only want you to know my feelings."

"Perhaps it's best you keep such feelings to yourself until you know my stance on things." Raziel shoved the bowl into his hands and said, "You can start proving yourself by ensuring that the community is properly fed." She walked away from the firepit and could feel Angelus' eyes on her as she left.

She didn't even think about where she was going to go. She started to walk toward the large gates and through them, heading toward the city on the beaten path. Raziel eventually hit the fork and kept walking toward the city. She was almost at the point where the foragers would meet someone to take them into the city when she saw the shrine built for Lily, Oriana, and Brian.

It was a large clearing, and two mounds of fresh dirt were surrounded by rocks outlining the graves. Raziel figured that sweet baby Oriana was buried with her mother; it was only fitting, and when she saw the burial spots, she dropped to her knees as tears poured from her eyes. Raziel's sorrow overtook her, and her entire body shook with anger and sadness. If she hadn't banished them, she wouldn't have been forced to change the rules and wouldn't be facing the feelings that she had about Angelus.

She leaned back so she could look directly up at the sky. "Lily, forgive me." Raziel screamed into the air. She felt heavy with emotion, and she threw her fists into the ground as the tears fell from her face. The night Oriana was born felt special; it felt sacred, and it connected them. Without them on Earth, Raziel felt as if a part of her were missing.

Raziel soon heard footsteps approaching, and she called back, "Leave me!"

The footsteps continued and stopped shortly behind her. Raziel looked over her shoulder and saw Angelus standing there.

Raziel groaned and asked, "What do you want?"

He stepped closer and said, "I am truly sorry for any offense that I've caused. I know I'm still new here, and there are rules to be followed. I wanted to apologize for stepping out of line."

"Okay, you've apologized. Now leave me alone." But

when he sat down beside her, she rolled her eyes. "You're not a very good listener, are you?"

Angelus chuckled. "Not really, but it wouldn't be a very smart move to leave the compound leader out in the wilderness by herself. I'll stay silent. I'll be ready when you're ready to leave."

Raziel dropped her head in frustration. She didn't feel like she could properly let out her emotions with the newest member around. She groaned again and stood up. "Let's go." She started to walk back to the compound, and Angelus hung back a short distance.

Good.

As they walked through the gates, Angelus called, "Are you going to be alright?"

Raziel curtly said, "Yes."

As she continued to walk away from him, she looked around. There was nowhere she could go without him or anyone else bugging her. Ramona was in her path, and she asked, "Raziel, are you alright?"

Raziel nodded and motioned for her to stay away. This day felt odd, and she didn't want to do anything or say anything that she would come to regret later on. Raziel walked toward her cabin. She knew it would give her the space that she needed, and everyone would get the hint.

As she walked away, Raziel shouted back, "I'm taking my meals inside the cabin!"

She could smell the roses as she approached her oasis. They were starting to bloom, and with the countless bushes, the scent was overwhelming. Raziel stormed into the cabin and threw herself onto her bed.

She let her eyes unleash the true fury and sorrow that she had been holding in. Raziel felt like her emotions were spinning out of control and were bringing her down with them. She wasn't sure how long she'd spent crying into her pillows, but eventually, she stopped, and when she turned her head to look out the window, the sun was already at its highest point in the sky.

Raziel sniffled and knew that she couldn't hide from her community for long, even though she wanted to and was contemplating it. Eventually, a soft knock sounded at the door. Raziel sighed, getting off the bed and going to unlock the door. Ramona was standing on the other side with a tray of food, a concerned look on her face as she whispered, "Raziel, we need to speak."

Raziel rolled her eyes and loudly said, "Fine."

Ramona entered the cabin and placed the platter on the bed while Raziel began to pace around the cabin.

Ramona sat on the bed and watched Raziel for a moment before Raziel abruptly broke the silence. "Do you think I'm stupid? Heartless?"

Ramona stared at Raziel in shock and stuttered out an answer. "N-no!"

Raziel stopped in the middle of the room and looked at Ramona. "Are you sure?"

Ramona bowed and took a deep breath in, as if she were preparing for some kind of backlash. "I've noticed how you've been a bit on edge lately, especially since Angelus—"

Raziel cut her off. "No, I know where you're going with this—"

"Do you, Raziel? Because we've never had an in-depth conversation about love or what you look for in a partner, and now that Lily, Brian, and Oriana are gone, we can tell that something is off."

Raziel took a step closer, and in a hushed tone, she seethed, "Who are *you* to question the will of gods?"

Ramona shook her head and let out a sigh. "Raziel, you're *not* a god. You're here on Earth with us, and while you're still our leader, we still have free will."

Raziel's eyes went wide, and her head fell back. She let out a loud cackle that threatened to shatter every window in the cabin. Ramona watched her and became uncomfortable with where the conversation was headed.

Raziel eventually stopped laughing and rushed toward Ramona. When she was just inches from her face, she whispered, "Don't you find my rose bushes lovely? The blooms are so plump and robust."

Ramona cautiously replied, "Yes, they are quite beautiful this year, but that isn't what I wanted to talk to you about, Raziel. Please, can we stay on topic?"

Raziel's eyes went into slits. "I cannot fall in love, Ramona. It's not possible."

Ramona stared at her in disbelief. "What are you talking about?"

The fallen angel smirked and said, "My curse is that I cannot fall in love. Angelus sparks something inside of me and makes me feel crazy."

"That sounds like love to me."

This caused Raziel to grip Ramona's shoulders and shake them slightly. "Ramona, you have *no idea* what you're talking about. Stop it!" She let Ramona go and started to pace again.

Ramona quietly asked, "Is your guilt so great that you changed the rules because of Lily? You blame yourself for their deaths?"

Raziel stopped walking and looked at her, simply nodding.

"It took you this long and three deaths to change the rules?"

Raziel scowled at her. "Everyone had been happy living in the free love society—"

"It wasn't a *true* free love society if people couldn't choose, though."

Raziel nodded again. "Exactly, which was why I changed it."

Ramona shook her head. "It took people *dying* for you to deem it worthy of changing. How many people have to die for you to change any other rules?"

Raziel's rage started to bubble under the surface. "What *other* rules would you want to change, Ramona?"

"I don't know, Raziel, but I'm saying that it's messed up—"

"You can leave."

Ramona stood up, and she walked across the cabin. As she gripped the door, she looked over her shoulder. "Something is wrong with you. I don't know what happened for you to become erratic like this, but you need to realize a few things before we can see you as our leader again."

Raziel ran over and grabbed Ramona by her hair, and she slammed her onto her back. Ramona let out a grunt as the air was knocked out of her lungs. Raziel climbed on top of Ramona and seethed, "I am *always* going to be your leader. It's because of *me* that all of you have this!"

Ramona turned her face and spat. "Bullshit, Raziel. Look at yourself right now!"

Raziel was beginning to see red as she said, "I would be very careful and watch the words that are coming out of your mouth, Ramona. I can kick you out, and I won't lose a moment of sleep over it."

Ramona looked up at her. "Do it, then. Banish me like all the others who stood up for the commune."

They stared at each other for some time before Raziel sighed and got off of Ramona. She walked over to the tray of food and hissed, "Get out! Someone else will bring me my meals. I don't want to see your face for the rest of the day."

Ramona rushed out of the cabin. Raziel slumped onto the bed, and in a fit of anger, she pushed the platter off. Dishes shattered under her feet, and the food was splattered all over the bed and up the wall.

Raziel sighed and fell back onto her bed. She ran her fingers through her hair and went over the conversation with Ramona. She knew where Ramona was coming from, and while part of her was angry for the insubordination, she knew there was some truth to what Ramona was saying. The rules had been in place since the beginning, and Raziel hadn't changed them for anyone… until Lily.

For the first time in a very long time, she felt like she wanted to end Nirvana. The humans were starting to drain her again, and she felt like her divinity was depleted. Raziel heard a *whooshing* sound, and she looked over to her side to see Natalia coming out of the small shadows in the corner.

Raziel sat up and sighed. "Natalia, I'm not in the mood for a meeting right now."

Natalia tiptoed around the spilled food, and she said, "Unfortunately, you don't have a choice. I got a tiny little nudge that told me I needed to be here. What's wrong with you?"

Raziel sighed and sat up. "I can't do this anymore…"

Natalia looked at her in confusion, and Raziel motioned around them. Natalia giggled and asked, "Oh, Sister, how come? Have the humans finally gotten to you?"

"They just take and take from me, and when I finally give them what they want, it's too late. Or they only focus on the negative situations that caused the changes."

Natalia walked over to the large Monstera plant in the corner, inspecting it. "What do you expect? Humans are overgrown babies. Of course, it's never going to be good enough. Of course, they are just going to continuously take from you and give nothing in return; they are selfish. You should know that by now."

Raziel stared at her feet, and Natalia inspected her nails. "You forget that we never turn our backs on the humans."

She looked up at her sister, and Natalia whispered, "Make them remember what you're capable of, Sister. Get your community back in line. *You* are in charge, not them." Raziel nodded, and Natalia pointed at her. "You're drained, but you know what needs to be done."

10

Natalia walked past her again and faded into the tiny shadows, disappearing from the cabin. Raziel felt something start to rise inside of her, and she stood up, snapped her fingers, and instantly, the dishes were reassembled, and the food was cleaned up. Raziel looked around, and when she was pleased with the clean-up, she changed into a blood red floor-length Grecian gown. It accentuated her curves perfectly and was just thin enough to see her body beneath it without being too revealing. She flipped her head over and fluffed her hair up again, and when she flipped it back, she was pleased with its volume.

Raziel left her cabin and walked to the main hall, where the great horn was located. She saw the chef walking toward her, and she called, "Can you prepare a big batch of your jungle juice?"

When the chef bowed to her request and walked away, Raziel blew the horn, indicating that a community meeting needed to be held. People began to come from all directions and walked toward her. As they approached in large groups, Raziel noticed them talking amongst themselves, and she lifted her head in slight defiance. The more people gathered in front of her, the more Raziel became confident that this was the right thing to do.

The entire commune filled the clearing, and before she began to speak, the kitchen staff brought out several large coolers, liquid sloshing in them as they moved and were set down beside Raziel. She looked out into the crowd and saw Angelus and Ramona's faces. She cleared her throat and looked at Ramona again, who was glaring at her. Raziel felt a pang in her chest, and it felt like her heart was breaking. She knew Ramona was disappointed in her, and Raziel wondered if there was any chance of reconciliation.

The more she looked into the crowd, the more she saw that there were several pairs of couples who had clearly jumped on the monogamous bandwagon. Raziel sighed as she felt the familiar feeling of jealousy start to rise inside of her. She couldn't help but think, *Why should they be happy in pairs? I offer them paradise. Why should they be able to fall in love while I simply get to experience pleasure? It's not fair!* The longer Raziel stared at her community, the angrier she became.

They all stared back at her, and she began to pick up the uneasiness that was spreading through the crowd. Raziel sighed; she was curious as to when they all started turning on her. It didn't seem like that long ago when they were all content just living by the rules.

She cleared her throat, and she loudly asked, "Are you unhappy here?" Her followers all exchanged glances, and she saw them shift uncomfortably. She said even louder, "I'm waiting for an answer. Someone speak up!"

A gentleman stepped forward, Leonard. He was one of the carpenters and had been at Nirvana for over twenty years. Raziel was shocked to see him come forward, and even more surprised when he said, "The rules, Raziel. You have never been one to change them, and now you give in at the smallest mishap."

"You think Lily's death was a small mishap?"

"Did you kill Lily yourself?"

Leonard and Raziel both gaped at each other, and the commune held their breath, waiting for Raziel's response.

Raziel shook her head slightly and said, "I'm the reason they left."

Leonard shrugged. "That might be, but they didn't follow the rules, and you held them accountable. It's not your fault that they couldn't make it into the city, to safety, in time." Raziel felt her eyes start to well up with tears as he continued, "The leader I knew, the one I loved and dedicated my life to, would stand her ground because she knew that the rules she implemented made Nirvana, well, Nirvana."

Raziel nodded, and as she looked around, she saw the couples start to pull away and continue to look at each other nervously. She said loudly, "I will not beat myself up for their deaths. As much as I miss them, it isn't my fault."

Leonard bowed and stepped back into the crowd. Raziel smiled at him, thankful for his support, and she looked out at everyone else and loudly asked, "Does anyone else have anything to say?" The silence was deafening.

Someone from the back cleared their throat, and Raziel shouted, "Speak up!"

Angelus stepped forward. Raziel's breath caught in her

throat, and with some disdain, and she said, "You haven't been here long enough to have an opinion."

Angelus shrugged. "That may be, but I still have a right to speak and to be heard."

Raziel shut her mouth, and she went to pour some of the jungle juice into one of the cups that she was handed by one of the kitchen staff. She gripped it with both hands and felt it start to warm up, and she saw the liquid glow slightly. Angelus watched her as she handed him the cup.

She smiled at him and said, "Drink, then speak." She smirked at him as he drank the entire thing in one long gulp and handed the cup back to her before turning to the crowd. "Nirvana isn't supposed to be a dictatorship; it's not even supposed to have a matriarchal system. It's supposed to be free. Free to love whomever, free to be yourself, and free from societal expectations and rules!" He pointed to Raziel. "She's still imposing rules, just under the guise of it being for the greater good."

Raziel was confused. Angelus should have snapped into line with the drink, and she looked out to the crowd, murmuring and agreeing with Angelus. Raziel coughed, and then said, "Well, let's welcome a new dawn in Nirvana with a toast. Everyone line up to get a cup!"

Every time she filled a cup, she transferred some of her divinity into the drink, enchanting every person to become obedient and wanting things to go back to how they were. She didn't know what happened with Angelus, but she was under the impression that she needed to watch him closer; something was *definitely* off about him.

Once everyone, including herself, had a cup in their hands, she raised hers and yelled, "To Nirvana!" And this caused the crowd to echo her. She watched as everyone took their first sip, and they all had the same shudder at the same time, as if they were being reset.

Ramona stepped forward and said, "Rules are in place to ensure that Nirvana runs smoothly!"

Raziel nodded and replied, "Thank you, Ramona. You're right."

Angelus looked around him, confused, and then turned his attention back to Raziel. He stepped forward again. "What happened to a *new dawn* in Nirvana? You were all so keen about it earlier."

Leonard yelled, "Don't like the rules? Get out of here!"

Angelus looked at Raziel, and there was an odd expression on his face. She avoided his eyes and clapped her hands together. "Well, shall we get everything ready for a meal?"

A sound of approval rippled through the crowd. Raziel was pleased, knowing that things were going to go back to normal. Before they all departed, Angelus tried once more, "Can we get a vote on the rules?"

He was met with disapproving glares, and someone from the back called out, "You're free to leave!"

Angelus looked at Raziel, who shrugged. Everyone broke off into smaller crowds, and the kitchen staff started to make their way back to the kitchen. Angelus approached Raziel, and she couldn't help but notice the misunderstanding on his beautiful face.

When he got close enough to her, he asked, "What just happened?"

Raziel stared at him, and she replied coolly, "The commune has spoken, Angelus."

She put both of her hands behind her back as she began to walk away, and heard him start to run after her.

"But how did that happen?"

Raziel stopped and looked at him as suspicion crept into her tone. "If I didn't know any better, I would think that you were trying to overthrow me, Angelus."

He looked to the ground and quietly said, "I just want to make Nirvana better."

Raziel glared at him. "Better?! Better than the oasis that I have dedicated my entire life to creating?"

Angelus looked up at her and replied, "Yes."

The sky above them began to darken as Raziel became increasingly angry, and she carefully whispered, "I suggest you choose your next words wisely."

Angelus sighed. "You know how I feel about you. I just want you to myself."

Raziel tilted her head slightly and thought for a moment as the sky started to light up above them again. She closed her eyes and whispered, "I am for everyone, Angelus. I am not only for one man or for one woman. That's the beauty of Nirvana, and if you cannot appreciate Nirvana for what it is, then perhaps this isn't the place for you." Raziel smirked at him and left.

He stood in the same spot and watched her walk away from him.

Raziel's heart was beating so fast that she was sure it would give her away. When she got back to her cabin, she slumped to the floor, trying to rationalize her swaying the community again. She knew that no one would truly understand what happened, but they would all be happy once more and go about their everyday lives and routines.

She sighed, and when she stood up again, she couldn't help but wonder why it didn't affect Angelus. She saw him drink from the cup! She wondered if she should contact Natalia about it, but Raziel knew that if she got Natalia involved with the atmosphere of Nirvana, it could ruin everything. She sighed. Maybe if she spent a bit more time with Angelus, she would be able to figure out what his angle really was.

As Raziel looked out the window, she saw that several of

the rose bushes were wilting. Her face scrunched up into a scowl. She quickly went outside, and as she walked through the garden, she saw the roses turning black. The smell that was coming from the garden was rancid, and Raziel recognized that it was the smell of rotting flesh.

She looked around. None of the bodies were exposed to the air, but it smelled as if she were right beside them. Raziel felt sick to her stomach; she knew she wouldn't be able to hide this from anyone in the compound. Dropping to her knees, she began to claw at the earth under one of the very first rose bushes that she had planted.

When she reached where she had placed the body, she was relieved to see that he was still there. He was almost reduced to his skeleton, and as she stared at the hand, the flashback of Timothy trying to organize an uprising flooded her mind. Raziel became angry once more, and she stared at the corpse.

"You deserve to rot here," she said out loud.

She stared at it, and for a moment, she thought that it had flinched ever so slightly, causing her to fall back in shock. Raziel looked around her, suddenly realizing how quiet it had become. She couldn't even hear voices in the distance or the birds above her; even the bugs had become silent. Raziel inched closer to the small hole and looked in again, relieved to see that Timothy was still dead, decomposing, and not moving.

She breathed, but she couldn't shake the feeling of doom that had suddenly overwhelmed her. Raziel, all of a sudden, felt like someone was going to find her graveyard. It would unravel everything that she had worked so hard on, and Nirvana would be destroyed. She knew that she needed to take protective measures, so Raziel began to separate the rose bushes and place them at the front of the garden, hoping that the fresh flowers would mask the smell and distract anyone from going closer to investigate.

Raziel spent the entire afternoon transferring rose bushes to other places around the garden, and when she was finished, it hit her that no one had bothered her the entire time. She stood up and looked around at her handiwork. She was pleased with her efforts.

She then looked down at herself, realizing how filthy she had become. Raziel walked around to the back of the cabin and started the water in her tub before placing the heater under it. As she turned on the water spout at the side to wash her hands, the water dripping turned from brown to crimson red, shocking Raziel. She looked at her hands and saw that they were dripping with blood, and the dirt that had covered her dress previously was now red and leaking from the skirt seams.

Raziel stared at her hands in horror. Every time she tried to wash the blood off, more seemed to drip from them. She closed her eyes tight, and when she opened them again, the bathtub was overflowing with red, bloodstained water. She started to slowly back away, and she screamed, "Enough!"

She blinked, and the blood had disappeared. Looking at her hands once more, they were stained brown from the soil, and her dress was almost black from the amount of dirt that it was saturated with.

Raziel looked around, her breathing rapid and her thoughts scattered. The soft bubbling of hot water started to sound as the liquid in her tub began overheating. She ran over and pulled the flame from underneath it and sighed. The water was boiling hot, but she undressed and stepped into the scorching tub anyway. Raziel hoped she could cleanse herself of what she had just witnessed.

She sank down into the water until she was completely submerged. Dunking her head under the surface, she held herself there until her lungs were threatening to burst from a lack of oxygen. When she sat up again, Raziel's skin was as red as if she had been in the sun for too long.

When she got out of the water, her skin was red and sore. She walked in through the back door and quickly braided her hair, and as she looked out the window, she saw that the sun was starting to set, and the smell of food cooking started to waft into her cabin.

As she left for dinner and walked past the garden, Raziel stopped and inhaled deeply. She was met with the sweet floral scent of the rose bushes. She stared at the garden, perplexed; she knew what she had smelled before. She would know the smell of decaying bodies anywhere, and she was confident that she had smelled it earlier. She was confused but continued to walk across the clearing to the dining hall. Raziel watched for any disturbances to indicate that her divinity transfer didn't go well.

When she walked into the eating area, she was greeted by the sounds of happy, carefree conversations running down the hall. No one paid her much attention as she entered the building, but she had the urge to eat alone anyway and wanted to process what she had witnessed at her cabin. As she was about to leave the building, she heard her name called, and she turned around to see Ramona coming toward her.

Raziel held her breath, expecting some kind of backlash, but as Ramona came closer, the look of concern was blatant on her face as she looked at Raziel's skin and asked, "Raziel! What happened?"

Raziel looked down at her very red arms. "I've been in the rose garden all day. The sun got to me."

Ramona bowed and replied, "I will harvest some aloe after dinner and come to apply it for you."

Raziel agreed, and then continued to walk out of the dining hall.

When she reached the lake, she set the plate down on the ground, and when she stood straight again, she closed her eyes, trying to calm her nerves. If things were going to go back to normal, she needed to change her attitude; she needed to be the carefree leader that they saw her as.

These past few weeks had been so chaotic and had affected her on a divine and molecular level. Raziel knew that she was the only one who could balance the community. While she felt depleted after transferring her intentions to her followers, Raziel knew she needed to focus again.

Leaving her plate on the ground, she walked out to the middle of the lake and sat cross-legged on the surface. She allowed herself to become immersed in the calmness of the water, surrounded by the sound of wings flapping and frogs singing their tunes. She finally felt herself becoming grounded as the nature around her consumed her. She released her stress, concerns, and fear into the Universe.

When she opened her eyes, the area around her was black, as if it had been consumed by a black hole. The water beneath her had turned to tar, and she had lost her focus; she plummeted into the depths of the lake. Raziel tried to reach the surface, but the harder she fought, the further she was pulled into the watery abyss. She felt her body start to resist taking a breath, her lungs beginning to burn, and she finally inhaled, causing everything to turn dark.

Raziel opened her eyes to see Angelus on top of her, breathing into her mouth. Both of them soaking wet, she began coughing, and all of the lake water that she had swallowed exited her body. Raziel sat up, alarmed, and looked around, the dusk providing a beautiful golden glow on the crystal-clear lake.

She shook her head, and she quietly asked, "Did you see that?"

She pointed out to the lake, but Angelus just looked at her. "Raziel, you fell into the lake. I got to you as soon as I could."

Raziel shook her head. "No, everything was black, dark, and the water was…" She trailed off when she saw the look of disbelief on his face.

She cleared her throat and thanked him for saving her. She then shakily stood up and walked over to the plate on the ground to pick it up. Raziel wasn't sure what was happening, but she didn't want Angelus anywhere near her while she figured it out.

11

As Raziel picked up her plate, she fell over. Angelus ran to her as she tried to stand up again.

"Raziel! Sit down, I mean it."

She glared at him and sputtered, "How is it that you always find me in my most vulnerable moments?" He pulled her back down and got her into a comfortable position. He still hadn't answered. Raziel said even more aggressively, "Angelus!" He looked up, and she asked him again, "How is it that you're always there?"

His eyes softened, and he whispered, "Call it a hunch? I just want to be there for you."

She scanned his face, and the image of her drowning in

the tar flashed in her mind. She jumped, and he stared deep into her eyes.

"Maybe we should go to the infirmary."

Raziel shook her head. "I just want to be alone, Angelus. Please leave me alone." He went to object, but she held her hand up. "I said leave, please." He knew better and didn't say another word as he stood up and left her staring out into the lake.

Raziel felt like her entire world was crumbling around her. She had never felt so out of control before, and she didn't know what to do. As her eyes welled up with tears, she knew she needed to contact Natalia.

Once she felt better, she stood up and was relieved to see that no one was near her. Raziel still thought that it was odd how Angelus just happened to be there. Sighing, she was grateful that, this time, he was.

Walking slowly to her cabin, Raziel felt nervous about contacting her sister. She was worried that she wouldn't come; Natalia could be slightly abrasive. As she opened the door, she was surprised to see Natalia sitting on her bed, inspecting her nails. Natalia looked over her hand as Raziel opened the door. She pointed with a finger and motioned up and down.

"What happened?"

Raziel crumbled and told her everything. Initially, Natalia had her legs crossed, but by the time Raziel finished, her older sister was leaning forward, a slight look of interest on her face.

They stared at each other for some time before Raziel finally said, "Natalia, say something!"

She watched as Natalia stood up and motioned for her to stand. When they were at eye level, Natalia reached out and placed her hand on Raziel's chest and quietly whispered, "Breathe."

Raziel took a deep breath in, and Natalia's hand began to glow a soft pink. They looked at each other, and as her hand grew warm, Raziel felt recharged and at peace.

Natalia pulled her hand back, and Raziel asked, "How did you know?"

Natalia smiled at her and replied, "I can always sense when you're spiraling. Next time, don't leave it for so long."

Raziel's brow furrowed. "This time was different though, Sister."

Natalia nodded. "I told you, there is another force walking this Earth right now. I don't know who they are or what they want, but Azazel is losing her mind, and I felt your shift. Keep your wits, Sister."

Raziel shook her head. "Something isn't right."

Natalia nodded and replied, "Whoever is here has tipped the balance." She pointed at Raziel and said, "Stay sharp. I mean it, Raziel." She turned back toward the darkness of the cabin and disappeared.

Raziel had enough of the day and decided to turn in for the night. Stripping off her soaking dress and placing it over one of the hooks on the wall, she changed into a pink gown and crawled into bed. Once she was covered and comfy, she pulled the sheets over her head and closed her eyes, waiting for sleep to consume her.

It didn't take long for her to fall asleep and back into the days at the garden. It was easy when there were only two humans in the entire world, and they were contained in one place. Raziel had always been convinced that there was more to the story than just the apple. She had kept her theories to herself for millennia, but when she fell back to Earth, she knew *exactly* how she wanted to model Nirvana. It was to be reincarnated in the image of Eden.

She'd worked so hard to keep everyone safe, happy, and satisfied.

Raziel was spinning around in the open space after she had just erected the walls, when suddenly, a large dark cloud floated over the top of the compound, threatening to pour down on her.

She looked up at the sky and screamed, "Smite me if you are so angry! Do it!" She had never defied the Creator in such a way before, but when she figured out how cruel, self-ish, and conceited He was, she was willing to do anything to reject and offend Him.

Raziel stared at the sky, repeatedly screaming to be struck down if He were indeed that offended. Eventually, the sky started to brighten, and the clouds began to open. She laughed and said to herself, "That's what I thought!"

As she turned her back, Raziel heard a crack, and when she looked back, a beam of white light was coming straight for her.

She sat straight up, screaming in her bed. Raziel felt all over herself; she began to cry as she realized that she was okay, and it was just a nightmare. She fell back into her pillows and tried to calm herself again. She needed to find out who this influence was. She needed to help Natalia set things right again, and if Azazel really was giving into her hunger, then it was only a matter of time before it got out of control again. If Azazel was spiraling even half as bad as Raziel was, that could mean total annihilation for Azazel's kingdom.

Raziel rolled over onto her side, a million thoughts running through her head.

She stayed awake until she saw the glow of the sun starting to creep into her cabin. She had spent the earliest hours of the morning thinking about the last time that Azazel needed to be reset, and it made her heart ache. As her cabin filled with sunshine, Raziel pulled herself out of bed and decided that she wanted a cold dip in the lake.

When she stepped out of the cabin, her breath was taken by the beauty that Nirvana offered in the morning. Before everyone woke up, the dew glistened on the grass, the birds flew low to get their breakfast, and chipmunks scurried around. Raziel grinned; the simplicity of these things was what made Nirvana so great, in her mind.

She got to the water's edge and was thrilled to see the sun reflecting off the water's surface. It gave the scene a euphoric glow, and it made Raziel excited to start her day. As she undressed, she pushed the images of her drowning the night before out of her mind.

Once Raziel was completely naked, she stepped into the water, which turned out to be a lot colder than she had anticipated. She kept walking into the depths, confident that no one would disturb her this early in the morning. Once the water was up to her shoulders, she dunked her head under, allowing herself to become cleansed by the water.

When she broke the surface once more, she wiped her eyes and saw naked Angelus entering the lake. She glared at him, furious that he had followed her again, and as he approached her, he started to glide through the water.

Once he got close to her, Raziel asked in an irritated tone, "What are you doing?"

Angelus smirked and replied, "Same thing you are, I suppose."

He went under the water and swam further into the lake. Raziel watched him and considered turning back; she hadn't accounted for anyone coming to disturb her peace.

While she wasn't embarrassed to be naked, Angelus made her feel vulnerable and exposed, and she wasn't sure if she liked it or not. She was shaken out of her thoughts when he swam closer to her again.

He quietly said, "I wasn't sure if you'd ever be able to get into the lake again."

Raziel tilted her head. "Water is healing. It cleanses your body and your soul. I'd be silly if I turned my back on it."

Angelus nodded. "I agree."

His eyes were so intoxicating that Raziel had to look away every few seconds; she feared that they would peek into her soul and see who she really was.

Angelus continued, "I am truly sorry if I offended you before. I feel called to follow you, comfort you, and care for you. I had an inclination that you have never had before."

Raziel's face scrunched up, and she said, "I have an entire community who cares for me."

Angelus shook his head and pulled himself even closer. "Not in the way that I want to take care of you."

Raziel looked at him and felt like her heart would beat out of her chest as he grabbed her gently and pulled her to his chest. He softly tilted her chin up and kissed her lips. It sent a current of electricity through her entire body and made her crumble at the same time. She melted into his embrace and allowed him to wrap his hands around her submerged waist. The two were lost in their passionate affair, lost in time, lost in each other.

When they pulled apart, Angelus whispered, "I know you felt that."

Raziel grinned and coyly whispered, "Shut up before I change my mind."

She pulled him back to her. Raziel's entire body was buzzing, and her mind was racing. She had never experienced these feelings before, and she heard Ramona's voice inside her head, "Lean into it." Raziel had spent her entire existence making sure that humans were taken care of and happy. It was finally her turn, and she refused to apologize for it.

After some time, they began to hear voices in the distance.

Angelus pulled away first and said, "I'll leave first. I'm sure you want to keep this quiet."

Raziel smiled at him and nodded. "Come find me later, though," she said reassuringly.

Angelus smiled back, swam to the edge, and got himself dressed quickly. With a look over his shoulder and a quick wave, he took off running toward the huts. Once he was out of sight, Raziel swam to the shallows and stepped out of the lake; her heart felt full. She knew that this was something special, a gift perhaps for staying on her path.

As she got dressed and walked back to her cabin, she was lost in the feelings of Angelus' mouth on hers. She had never tasted a kiss so sweet. Once she was inside, she shook her hair out, allowing it to flow freely around her body. Raziel felt light, and like she would float away if she allowed herself to lose herself in her feelings.

When she stepped out of her front door, she smelled breakfast and was excited for the food. This day had so much promise already, and Raziel was excited to see what else it had in store for her. When she reached the dining hall, she was greeted with the smell of a full scrambled egg breakfast and fresh fruit bowls. She grabbed a plate with sausage, fruit, eggs, and some toast. Out of nowhere, she became famished.

Raziel then walked over to the table that had all of the pregnant women and asked them how they were doing. She loved being able to feel the growing lives in their bellies. After her blessings, they all began to eat. Raziel was surprised that even the food tasted better. Every time Raziel looked over to his table, she saw Angelus staring at her. She would blush and look away, but she couldn't ignore the hunger that she saw in his eyes.

Raziel kept thinking about their moment at the lake; she kept touching her lips in between bites at the thought of Angelus' lips on hers. She started getting lost in her thoughts, and finally, someone grabbed her arm, and she noticed that the entire table was empty.

She looked up and saw Angelus. She beamed and quietly said, "Hi."

He kissed her cheek and asked, "Would you like to go for a walk?"

He motioned toward the gates, and Raziel enthusiastically agreed. Once they were outside, Angelus grabbed her hand, and they walked down the path, further into the jungle.

When they were quite a distance away, Angelus looked around and whispered, "This is the perfect place."

Then he turned his attention to Raziel, and she couldn't stop staring at him. When he took a step closer to her, Raziel became nervous.

Angelus tucked some of her hair behind her ear and whispered, "You're beautiful."

Raziel blushed and replied, "You're too kind."

Angelus shook his head and continued, "You are a *goddess.*"

Raziel looked at him, unsure if he'd meant to use that term, but then he kissed her, and she forgot any feelings of apprehension that she had before.

Angelus picked Raziel up effortlessly and carried her over to a thick tree so that her back was against the trunk. As he kissed down her neck, he whispered, "I needed to get you deep into the forest so no one would hear you."

He ran his hands up the outside of Raziel's thighs, and a fire ignited inside of her. She kissed him passionately and bit his bottom lip. Angelus let out a low growl, and the two of them gave in to their most primal needs, spending the entire morning deep within the forest, and ultimately, lost in each other.

Eventually, they decided that it was time to go back to

Nirvana. They walked back slowly with their fingers entwined with each other.

As they approached the gates, Angelus leaned in for one last kiss and said, "I'll come to you tonight if you want."

Raziel nodded and grinned as she said, "Please."

Angelus smiled one last time and walked through the gates. She watched him walk away, and as he was about to go over the slight hill, he looked over his shoulder and winked at her.

Raziel felt like she could fly. It was the most beautiful, passionate, and intense experience that she had ever had with a human, and it felt like it was just for her.

Suddenly, she heard her name being called, and when she spotted where the voice was coming from, Ramona was running toward her with a giant smile and a plate filled with food.

When Ramona got close enough, she giggled. "Raziel, you are absolutely glowing today! Could it have anything to do with Angelus?" Raziel's eyes went wide, and she went to object, but Ramona shook her head. "I saw the two of you at the lake this morning."

Raziel's mouth dropped, and she felt her face flush. Ramona smiled knowingly and said, "Let's go have lunch inside your cabin. I could use some tea."

The two of them continued walking to Raziel's cabin, and when they were behind the closed door, Ramona set the tray down onto her bed, and Raziel went to grab her kettle and cups.

Ramona sat on the bed, and she looked at Raziel innocently. "Well?"

This caused Raziel to reveal everything that had happened in the jungle. By the time she had poured the tea into the cups, she finished the entire story, causing Ramona to squeal in delight. Raziel was smiling the whole time, and Ramona pointed at her.

"I like this look on you."

Raziel looked down at the teacup as she handed it to her friend, and she nodded. "I like it, too." She sat beside Ramona, and she whispered, "He scares me, though, in a weird but wonderful way."

Ramona popped a tangerine slice into her mouth as she answered, "Love will do that."

Raziel shook her head. "It's not love, Ramona."

"It sure sounds like it! And you've been doing this back and forth with your feelings about Angelus since he got here. It's okay to give in to them; no one is going to stop you."

Raziel grabbed a grape and ate it thoughtfully. Ramona sighed slightly and asked, "Would you be okay with Angelus taking multiple partners?"

Raziel quickly looked at Ramona, and she felt like she had been stabbed in the heart. It hurt her to think of Angelus touching someone else like he'd touched her, to think of him kissing other people like he'd kissed her. She shook her head. "I don't think I would be."

Raziel felt confused, and she was trying to keep her feelings under the surface but couldn't deny them any longer. Ramona smiled knowingly, and she popped a strawberry into her mouth. After she was finished, she said, "That's love, Raziel."

12

Raziel looked at Ramona in shock and shook her head. "That's impossible, literally impossible!"

Ramona smiled and nodded reassuringly. "That's what we all say."

Raziel sighed and stood up. "No, Ramona; it is absolutely *impossible* for me to fall in love. It's a curse. I can watch others experience it, and I might come close to it, but I will *never* truly experience it."

"Why?"

"It's my punishment for my part in the uprising that caused the fall."

When Raziel looked back at Ramona, she saw Ramona's

shocked face. Raziel rarely, if ever, talked about the fall with her community. After the initial explanation when Nirvana opened, the story had been passed down through the followers so that Raziel would never need to retell it.

Ramona had never heard Raziel talk about it firsthand, and the look on her face was full of awe and wonder.

Raziel sighed and said, "You see? There's no way."

Ramona shook her head. "Everything you described is everything that I have felt any time I have ever been in love."

Raziel started to play with her hair, and she felt confused. "Ramona, I felt so connected to him."

Ramona bowed. "As if you were one."

Raziel nodded as Ramona stood up and started to pace around the cabin. She looked at Raziel and said, "If it's not love, then what is it?"

Raziel sighed and answered, "Infatuation that will turn into obsession if I don't cater to it."

Ramona shook her head. "No, I have seen you infatuated with people in the past, and I have never seen you act like this with anyone else for as long as I have been here."

They both stared at each other in silence until Raziel sighed and picked up the tray. "Okay, enough of that. Let's finish this platter." They continued to eat in silence, and Ramona let Raziel eat stress-free.

Once the platter was clean, Ramona cleared her throat and quietly asked, "When are you going to see him again?"

Raziel slowly smirked as she whispered, "He's going to spend the night tonight."

"Raziel, you're going to be spending the night with him, and after today in the jungle and this morning at the lake, you're telling me that it's not some form of love?"

"It could be a very mild form of it, I suppose, but if this is only a mild form of it, I don't know if I would be able to handle full-fledged love."

Ramona nodded. "It can be very intense."

The two women stared at each other intensely, and a deep cough interrupted them. Raziel looked behind them and saw Angelus approaching them. She smiled as Ramona took her leave. When he got close to Raziel, he kissed her cheek. She pulled away a little as she looked around to see if anyone was near them, and Angelus picked up on her signal.

Taking a step back, he quietly asked, "Are you ready for dinner?"

Raziel nodded, and he motioned toward the opening. "After you."

The two of them walked into the dining hall and saw that everyone was too preoccupied with their own meals to pay any attention to her and Angelus. They each grabbed their dishes and parted ways as Angelus went off to sit with the builders. Raziel sat with Ramona and some of the other women, and they all spoke about the upcoming event, the harvest celebration. Raziel had almost forgotten that it was quickly approaching.

The foragers all went into town at the perfect time, and it was almost time for autumn to come. They spent a whole week giving thanks to the Universe, leading up to the full harvest moon. Raziel smirked, knowing that another full moon celebration was coming.

But she couldn't help but let her mind wander to how she and Angelus would celebrate. After dinner, it was suggested that a bonfire be created, and Raziel couldn't agree more that it would be a perfect way to end the day. Word spread throughout the hall, and once dinner was over, the commune split up, some to get the firepit ready while others went to grab warmer clothes for the fire starters.

Raziel decided on a thicker blanket, and she went to the firepit to oversee the creation. She was pleased to see that there was already a large fire started by the time she reached the pit. Angelus was heading the group and dictating the jobs that needed to be done next. Raziel suddenly felt complete, as if he were truly the piece of her that she had been missing.

He noticed her and smiled. When she smiled back, he motioned for her to come closer, and as she did, Raziel's heart began to race violently once more.

Once she reached his side, Angelus looked around and lowered his voice. "So, when would you like to sneak off."

Raziel smirked and replied, "Let's wait until *after* the campfire."

Angelus bowed, and she noticed a slight look of disappointment on his face but knew that she would make it up to him later. They both watched the flames grow higher, and as more people started to gather around, Raziel pulled away from Angelus and began to mingle with the other members.

After a long night of singing songs, telling stories, and roasting marshmallows, everyone began to disperse for bed. There were still a few members who were watching the flames die down as Raziel decided to take her leave. She made sure to make solid eye contact with Angelus as she left.

Raziel got back to her cabin and started to light candles around her room. It wasn't long before she heard a gentle knock on the door.

"Come in!"

"Wow, this is beautiful!" Angelus exclaimed as he entered the hut.

Raziel looked around, and she felt an overwhelming sense of gratitude. "It really is, isn't it?"

They looked at each other and instantly ran into each other's arms. Their bodies melted into one another, and they spent the entire night giving into lust.

Raziel wasn't sure when they passed out, but eventually, she found herself in a pitch-black forest. She felt like she needed to walk forward, but with every step she took, a growl began to sound off in front of her. She felt the pit of her stomach start to get more intense the closer she got. She couldn't see where the sound was coming from, but it began to come from behind her the further she walked. With her final step, it sounded like it was *right behind her*.

She gasped, and it felt like someone had pushed her over a cliff. She was falling into the abyss, and her arms were flailing in the air around her, reaching for anything that could help her. Raziel felt like she was going to crash into the ground, and the longer she fell, the faster she fell. Just as she was about to crash, she heard Angelus' voice. He was laughing, and it sounded like he was whispering into her ear. He was saying every name of the people whom she had killed and buried in her garden. As she hit the ground, she woke up.

Raziel sat straight up and looked around. Angelus was *gone*. She panicked and rushed out of bed. When she looked out her side window, she was relieved to see that the garden was empty, but she felt slightly vulnerable, waking up alone. It was still dark outside, and she climbed back into bed. She was sad that Angelus would leave after the incredible night they had just had. Raziel rolled over onto her side and closed her eyes, trying to keep her disappointment at bay so she could fall asleep again.

This time, when she fell asleep, she didn't dream once. When she woke up to the sun, Raziel felt like she had been awake all night. It was heavy exhaustion filled with sadness and regret. She got out of bed and got dressed. She then braided her hair and tried to keep her face neutral as she stepped out of the cabin.

People were already walking around with breakfast, and Raziel started to get a little pep in her step as she got closer to the dining hall. As she grabbed her food, she looked around and still saw no sign of Angelus. Even as she ate,

Angelus was missing, and Raziel knew that something wasn't right. The builders even came around, saying they were looking for him, and she began to grow concerned.

"How did last night go?" Ramona came over seconds later and asked.

Raziel groaned and quietly told her everything. Ramona stared at her, shocked as she said that he left in the middle of the night.

Raziel finished by bitterly asking, "Still believe it's true love?"

Ramona shook her head in disbelief. "No, there needs to be a reasonable explanation for this. I'm sure it's totally innocent."

Raziel rolled her eyes. "I think we both just got caught up in it, and I thought it was more serious than what it really was."

They sat in silence as Raziel finished her breakfast, and as she stood up, Ramona quietly said, "You're wrong, Raziel. I saw the two of you; I saw how you both looked at each other. You weren't imagining things or overthinking anything. Sometimes, those feelings are overwhelming, especially for men. Give him time. I'm sure he'll be back."

Before Raziel could disagree, Ramona stood up and left Raziel by herself. Raziel felt terrible, and now she felt worse; she hated this part of human emotions. The negative ones were so heavy and felt like they were suffocating.

As she walked out of the dining hall, she heard whispers of people asking where Angelus was, and she tried to ignore them; even the sound of his name left an awful taste in her mouth. She felt betrayed, allowing herself to be his for the day and allowing herself to feel vulnerable while he provided a safe space for her. If he ever came back, he was going to have to face her wrath, and she vowed that she wouldn't go easy on him.

Raziel spent her day overlooking different tasks around the compound. The cabin was coming to a beautiful finish, regardless of not having Angelus around to head their progress. As the lunch bell rang, Raziel started to walk toward the dining hall, and as she walked over the small hill, she saw the entire community surrounding *something*. Curious, Raziel began to run, and the closer she got, she realized that it was Angelus whom they were gathered around.

Her curiosity was instantly replaced with rage, and she stormed toward the group as people began to part for her. When she reached the center of the circle, she was surprised to see Angelus holding the most beautiful bouquet of red roses that she had ever seen. Raziel stopped and looked at him as he approached her to hand them to her.

"What are these for?" she asked.

Angelus smiled and replied, "For being an incredible inspiration to us all. I feel like I can speak for all of us when I say that we all strive to be even half of what you are so effortlessly."

Raziel searched the crowd and found Ramona's eyes, and she wished they could speak telepathically. She turned her attention back to Angelus, and she smirked. "Well, this is very sweet of you. Where did you get them?"

A sneer washed over his face as he said, "From your garden."

A collective gasp sounded, and people began to walk away hurriedly. Ramona was pulled aggressively by other members of the kitchen staff, and Raziel tilted her head as she threatened and asked, "What?"

Angelus bowed and replied, "Yes, I noticed how plump the flowers were, and I figured there was no better gift than the most beautiful flowers for the most beautiful woman."

Panic and anger started to breathe deep inside of Raziel,

but she collected herself. "I looked for you all day and didn't see you anywhere."

"I took the flowers early this morning out of Nirvana to fully prepare them. I didn't want anyone to see what I was doing." He smiled at her, and his eyes began to twinkle.

Raziel looked down at the flowers, and the only thing she could smell was decay. Angelus waited for her to say something, but she simply looked at him and said, "Do *not* go into my garden again." She began to walk away from him, but Angelus chased after her.

"Raziel! What did I do?"

She stopped and glared at him. "Don't go into my garden, Angelus."

He tilted his head. "Why?"

"It's private."

They stared at each other for a few moments before he stepped toward her, lowered his voice, and asked, "Because of all the corpses?"

Raziel's eyes grew wide, and she hissed, "Excuse me?"

Angelus smirked. "I said, because of the dead bodies buried beneath the bushes?"

Raziel felt like her stomach fell to her knees, and she tried to deny it. "I have no idea what you're talking about."

But Angelus smiled wider. "No? Shall we go see what I'm talking about? I wouldn't want you to be framed for someone else's murder."

"Who are you?!"

Angelus looked around them, and he snapped his fingers. Everything around them suddenly stopped, and when Raziel looked for the humans around her, they had all frozen in their places.

Angelus stretched his arms out to his sides, and a pair of elegant white wings spread from his shoulder blades. Raziel took a step back and stared at him in horror. Angelus' skin started to glow ever so slightly, and Raziel was almost blinded by his ethereal beauty.

He held his hands up and said, "I'm not going to kill you. I was sent to observe… for now."

Raziel felt sick, and she shook her head. "No, no, this is a dream! It has to be! There's no way you're here!" She screamed, and he took a step forward.

"Do you really think the Creator would be able to forgive you and your sisters' violent tendencies toward His pets?"

Raziel shot him a nasty look with all the hate inside her body. "I don't care what His opinion is," she answered curtly.

Angelus smirked. "He said you would say something like that." He sighed and took another step forward. "Did you enjoy the games we played? Did you think you were going crazy? I know I did." The look on his face made Raziel's skin crawl.

She threw the flowers onto the ground, and she spat at him. "What now?"

Angelus shrugged. "I haven't gotten any further orders yet. Do you think the humans would rise up against you and take over Nirvana if I told them that you killed their family members to nurse your ego?"

Raziel lifted her head slightly. "They love me."

Angelus replied, "Let me guess, they get sick of your rules, mention they want change, and then you influence them back in line, forcing them to surrender to your wants and narcissism."

Raziel finally understood everything. Trying to keep herself as calm as possible, she looked around them and asked, "What do you want, Angelus?"

He innocently answered, "To watch you suffer. You have no idea how horrible it's gotten up there since you and your sisters ruined everything and sent Him on a warpath, taking

His anger out on the angels left. I was sent to ensure that you pay for it."

Raziel looked at him skeptically. "Well, looks like you ruined your own plan, now that I know who you are."

Angelus sneered at her wickedly. "Don't you worry your pretty little head about it." He raised his fingers and snapped.

Raziel sat straight up in bed and looked around in the darkness. Angelus was sleeping soundly beside her. She could feel herself shaking but couldn't figure out why. Leaning back against her pillows, she snuggled into Angelus' back and drifted back to sleep, her dreams foggy and unclear.

When she woke up in the morning, she felt like something was off.

Angelus rolled over and smiled at her. "Good morning."

Raziel gave him a small smile and replied, "It is."

He stretched his arms out and whispered, "Stay here. I'm going to get us some breakfast. Let's stay in today."

Raziel nodded. She felt like she had already lived the day once before, but it was different, like a dream that felt real. Raziel couldn't sort the thoughts out in her head, and she couldn't quite put her finger on it, but she felt different after Angelus had left the cabin.

Angelus soon returned with a large platter of fruit and a cheery disposition. He handed her the platter, and when she took it, he asked, "You alright?"

Raziel looked at him cautiously. "I'm not sure. I feel off."

He nodded. "Sometimes that will happen when you've connected with someone the way we have." He reached forward to tuck a strand of hair behind her ear, and when he touched her, Raziel felt repulsed.

13

Raziel tried to hide her disgust.

"I guess I can't get rid of all your hesitation, but I want to try." Angelus looked down at the platter. "How about you stay here, and I will go oversee how things are going out there? Take your time coming out."

Angelus leaned forward and kissed her on the forehead. Raziel felt like she was going to puke and stepped back slightly, nodding. "Okay, I'll see you out there."

Once he left, Raziel sat on her bed and slowly ate the fruit. She couldn't figure out what she was feeling. When she stood up, something caught the corner of her eye, and when she turned to look, she saw a large group of community members walking toward her cabin. Many of them had torches, and she watched in horror as one of them threw a torch into her garden. The bushes went up in flames, and Raziel ran out the front door to a mob of angry Nirvanians.

A man shouted, "Murderer!" The others echoed him.

Raziel held her hands up, trying to calm them down, but then the unmistakable stench of burning, rotting flesh filled the air around them. Raziel's eyes widened as everyone realized what it was.

Angelus came through the crowd and said, "I told them how you've been fertilizing your beautiful garden."

All of a sudden, Raziel remembered everything, and as she was about to scream, he snapped his fingers, and everyone was silent, still, and time had stopped. He walked around different members, and he called out, "It looks like I was right about their reaction!" He chuckled. "How long do you think it would take for them to kill you?"

Raziel violently shook her head. "Impossible."

Angelus sneered. "Maybe, but they sure would relieve a lot of frustration trying!"

"Enough, Angelus! Enough!"

He had a smug look on his face. "Oh, sweet Raziel, we are just getting started. I'll be in touch." He snapped his fingers again, and Raziel woke up in bed.

She looked around and began to panic. She remembered everything and knew she needed to get ahead of it. As she got out of bed, Raziel realized how much she was shaking. The sun was shining brightly through her windows, and she quickly got dressed.

Raziel ran toward the dining hall, where the kitchen staff was preparing breakfast. Without answering any of their questions, Raziel went over to the large containers of pink juice and placed her hands on them. The only thing that washed over her mind was *death*. The liquid began to bubble and turn into a lime green color. Raziel knew she needed to erase any memory of Angelus. When she took her hands away, she felt better.

She looked back to the staff and asked, "Can you bring these out? I have an announcement to make."

Raziel felt a twinge of guilt for interfering with her humans again, but she needed to protect Nirvana. As she walked out of the kitchen, she began calling everyone to gather around for her announcement.

"Come in close, everyone! I have an important message."

They all looked at each other and murmured amongst themselves. As the kitchen staff brought out the liquid, people began to get excited. Raziel heard whispers of *sour apple* or *limeade*, knowing that it was a group favorite.

"Shouldn't we wait for Angelus?" someone called out.

Hearing his name made Raziel feel ill. She shook her head and replied, "Angelus will have his when he returns." She looked around the compound as far as she could see, and when she didn't see any sign of him, she began talking to her followers.

She took a deep breath and said, "Brothers, sisters." She looked around as people stared back at her. "We are on the verge of something truly amazing here at Nirvana, and all of you are on the precipice of greatness, to go down in history as the *only* true free-loving society. Being a part of Nirvana is more than just being here in body; it's about truly immersing your soul into the essence of Nirvana." She felt the atmosphere start to soften as she motioned to everyone to start drinking from their cups. "Please, everyone. Drink, and then we shall all be merry." She looked around and took one of the cups, handing it to the chef. "I want you to take part as well."

He took it from her and greedily gulped it down. As Raziel attempted to start talking again, she noticed that someone in the back was starting to convulse and foam at the mouth. His eyes rolled into the back of his head, and he collapsed. Soon, everyone in the group began to shake, and they all dropped to the ground.

Raziel shook her head; this wasn't what she'd wanted! She rushed over to Ramona's side. Blood was starting to trickle from Ramona's nose, and she looked up in fear as Raziel held her.

Tears streamed down Raziel's cheeks, and she screamed, "No! No! This wasn't supposed to happen!" Ramona started to gurgle and made an attempt to speak, but Raziel shushed her and whispered, "Save your strength."

The entire compound took exactly seven minutes to succumb to death, and finally, Raziel stood up. She felt a hint of immense sadness when she saw the future mothers clutching onto each other. Raziel fell to her knees and let out a screech that shook the ground beneath her.

She bent over and began to sob into the grass. In the distance, she heard the sound of faint whistling, and when she popped her head up, she saw Angelus walking toward her. Raziel was filled with rage, and she stood up.

But before she could take a step, Angelus was right in front of her, and she screamed, "What did you do?!"

"I didn't do this, Raziel. You did."

He pointed at her, and she quickly shook her head. "No, no! I didn't mean to. I would *never* want to hurt them!"

There was a pleading undertone in her voice, and Angelus sucked the air through his teeth. "Has it crossed your mind that divinely influencing your following would have repercussions at some point? Perhaps humans are just meant to live out their pathetic little lives until it's time for cosmic judgment? Maybe we aren't to interfere because it gets to a point where the weak humans can't take it?"

"I know it's because of you," she denied. "Ever since you landed on Earth, everything has—"

He interrupted her. "Now, now, don't go blaming your shortcomings on me. There has *always* been something wrong with you and your sisters, trying to get the Creator to go against His own plan for the humans, trying to give the humans free will and further their learning." Angelus started laughing. "I can't believe you killed your entire following!" He looked around them. "Being on Earth really *has* made you lose it, huh? The Creator is going to be absolutely furious, and I can't wait to see what He unleashes on you and your pathetic fallen sisters."

Raziel felt hopeless; she couldn't believe she had just killed all of her beloved community.

She looked up at Angelus. "You can turn back time."

Angelus nodded. "Yes, I can."

Raziel continued, "You can fix this. You can bring them all back to life."

Angelus nodded again. "Yes, I can."

Raziel pleaded, "Please, bring them back. Please." Desperation was seeping from Raziel's entire body, and she felt empty as Angelus shook his head.

"Absolutely not."

Tears began to flow from her eyes again, and she let out a sorrowful howl. Angelus watched her in pure glee, and he looked around the entire compound. "So, what are you going to do with the compound now? You can't cover the ground in rose bushes." He chuckled as he began to walk away from her.

Raziel felt a rage inside her that she had never felt before, and she stood up quickly, chasing after him. But Angelus turned around quickly, grabbed her by the neck, and slammed her to the ground when she got closer.

"You've been on Earth for far too long, and I promise you

that your powers aren't even a faint whisper to what mine are. I suggest you stay on the ground."

He let go of her neck, and she asked, "What are you going to do?"

Angelus walked away from her and yelled back, "You'll know when it happens."

He disappeared and left her staring at her fallen family members. All of a sudden, she heard her name being screamed, and she looked back and saw Natalia walking toward her, a look of utter shock on her face.

"Sister, what happened?!"

She looked around, and Raziel answered, "I lost it. I lost control. Angelus, one of our new members. He's an angel."

Natalia looked at Raziel and sarcastically said, "Oh, really? A man named Angelus was an angel? Shocker, Raziel."

Raziel always hated Natalia's sarcasm, but even she couldn't help but agree with her sister. She had let her feelings control the outcome instead of using her head. Raziel looked around, and Natalia sighed. "This is a serious mess; you understand that?"

Raziel nodded. "How do we fix it?"

Natalia started to maneuver through the bodies. "We are going to bury everyone, and you're not going to allow *anyone* into Nirvana for at least a hundred years. That way, we can be absolutely sure that the bodies will be completely dissolved into the earth."

Raziel bobbed her head slowly, and Natalia clapped her hands. "Well, let's do this."

Raziel felt her eyes start to fill with tears again, and Natalia shook her head. "Sister, no. Don't start; they are *just* humans. Pull yourself together!"

Natalia lifted her hands, and the bodies started to sink into the ground. They were underneath the surface in mere seconds, and wildflowers had begun to sprout up in their place. Natalia glanced around, and then confidently said, "See, that's so much better."

Raziel sighed. "I feel so heavy, Sister."

"I know, but you need to pull yourself up out of your sadness. We have bigger issues at hand."

Raziel looked up at her and saw Natalia looking into the distance. She then looked over her shoulder and saw Angelus walking toward them.

Natalia lowered her voice and whispered, "I see why you were so distracted, Sister; he is scrumptious."

Angelus stood before them and said, "Ladies."

Natalia scoffed. "They sent the poster child down here?"

Raziel looked at Natalia in confusion. "You know him?"

Natalia shook her head slightly. "Barely. He was entry-level while we were doing all the hard work."

Angelus smirked. "And then when the three of you had your grace and wings ripped from you, I had the honor of carrying the brunt of the rage that filled Heaven."

Natalia rolled her eyes. "Oh, the tragedy plays that they could write about your sorrowful life."

Angelus glanced at Raziel. "I should have just killed *her* instead of wasting my time with *you*."

Raziel stood up. "Angelus, you're a *yes man*. You won't act until you have orders."

Angelus nodded. "Yes, you're right. But I was able to almost drown you in your own lake. I was able to convince your own followers to almost kill you. And I didn't have orders to do that, so I suggest we all play nicely, or I *will* act accordingly."

Natalia and Raziel exchanged looks, and Natalia spoke, "So, cut the chase. Stop wasting our time. What is it that you want?"

Angelus replied, "The Creator wanted to know if you

three had changed and were worthy of getting back into Heaven."

Raziel shook her head. "No, you're mistaken. We were told that there would *never* be a chance of that happening." Natalia nodded in agreement.

Angelus shrugged. "I'm only relaying the information that I have."

Natalia smirked. "Well, I think you got something confused because we were told that there is no way that we could ever come back."

The three of them stared at each other, and Angelus asked, "Where's Azazel?"

Natalia shrugged. "Don't know."

He looked at her skeptically. "You don't know?"

Natalia shook her head. "She has put her own divinity into protecting her kingdom. Azazel doesn't show up until she *wants* to show up."

Angelus smiled widely. "Right, and the divine source for the fallen trio has no idea where one of her dependents is."

Raziel felt nervous, and she could sense that Natalia was reaching her last nerve as she said, "Look, I'm getting bored with you, your empty threats, and watching you harass my sister. Either you leave us be, or you get on with it and try to kill us."

Angelus bowed. "Ladies, I shall be back."

As he left, Natalia looked back at Raziel and said, "He's kind of an asshole, yeah?"

Raziel nodded. "This was nothing. His power is truly something else."

Natalia studied her sister's face, and she solemnly said, "You're going to tell me everything that happened."

Raziel nodded and began telling her everything, from Angelus arriving to the blood dripping off of her like a fountain when she started a bath, from drowning in the lake that had turned to tar to Angelus turning back time. When she finished with the mob coming to get her, Natalia's face was as white as the clouds in the sky.

Natalia was quiet for a moment, and then she said, "We need to hide Nirvana. Blanket it so he can't get back in or find you once I leave."

"What?! You can't leave!"

"I have my own kingdom to look after, and I need to check on Azazel."

Raziel shakily said, "Fine, but promise to come back to check on me regularly. I mean it."

Natalia nodded. "I promise, Raziel. I'll check in constantly." She grabbed Raziel's hands. "I absolutely promise you."

Raziel stood up, and the two of them joined hands. They closed their eyes, and Raziel imagined a dome being lowered over the Kingdom of Nirvana. Once she felt like it had surrounded the entire compound, Natalia dropped her hands and pulled her into an embrace.

"I'm sorry this happened to you, Sister. I'm sorry you were tricked by an awful man."

"I thought it was love, Natalia. I feel so stupid."

Natalia sighed. "They have a tendency to do that." She pulled away from Raziel and said, "You are a fallen angel, a goddess on Earth. Remember who you are, heal yourself, and get him off of our radar." Raziel nodded. "Walk me back to the shadows. I will be back in a few days to see how things are going. I want to observe Azazel." Natalia studied Raziel's face for a few more minutes. "You're going to be okay, Raziel. Everything is going to be alright. Now that we know who we're dealing with, I won't let anything happen to you or to Azazel."

Raziel scoffed. "The fact that you have to observe Azazel just goes to show how unstable we are, Natalia."

Raziel looked around to where the bodies were and felt

her sadness swell once more. She still couldn't believe that she had caused the massive death of her people.

Natalia sighed. "Well, Sister, I do believe that you are experiencing true heartbreak. You truly did love everyone here, and the only way to heal is to mourn. Do whatever you need to do so you feel better, Raziel, but *do not* stay in that mindset; it will kill us all."

When they walked back to Raziel's small hut, Natalia turned to her and gripped both of her sister's shoulders. "Sister, it's going to be just fine. In a hundred years, no one will even begin to remember what happened here, and you can start advertising Nirvana as the oasis it is again. Spend time bettering it, even though I doubt it's possible."

Raziel smiled at Natalia weakly. She just wanted her sister to leave so she could be alone.

Natalia picked up on it, so she finally said, "Sister, I'll see you in a few days. You're stronger than you're giving yourself credit for."

Raziel looked into Natalia's eyes and saw that she meant it. She nodded, and she turned to leave the cabin as Natalia disappeared into the faint shadows in the corner.

When Raziel walked out into the open space, she felt how empty the compound now was. Looking around, she was able to hear the birds chirping and the frogs croaking down by the lake. It was serene but incredibly sad. She breathed and decided that she would build the largest funeral pyre in Nirvana's history.

She spent two days and two nights building the large wooden structure, and then went on to carve the name of every member who had perished into it. When she carved Ramona's name, Raziel screamed out in anguish, and her guilt consumed her. She sat on the ground and sobbed until she felt like she had been depleted of any moisture left inside her body.

It started to get dark, and she gathered herself once more and continued to carve Ramona's name and finished everyone else's names. Once darkness fell over the commune, she lit the structure on fire. As the smoke drifted up to the sky, she sent her anger and sorrow with it.

14

Raziel wasn't sure when she fell asleep, but she opened her eyes to the sunshine blinding her. She was covered in dew, and when she looked at the structure, it had been reduced to ash. She stood up and saw the coals glowing, and her sorrow became the tiniest twitch in her heart. Raziel knew that the next one hundred years could either go as slow or as fast as she allowed it to, and if she stayed in her sadness, it would feel like an eternity.

As she continued to immerse herself in her thoughts, she heard a loud bang, and it felt like Nirvana shuddered. Raziel looked around, and she heard the deafening sound once more; it was coming from the gates. She walked over and opened them, and she was surprised to see Angelus on the other side.

Raziel raised a brow and called out, "Something wrong?"

She saw him chuckle, and he replied, "Seems like Nirvana is invite-only now."

"Yeah, and you're not on the list."

Angelus looked up and around him. "Is this powered by Natalia?"

Raziel shrugged. "Not sure. It just appeared."

"You know I can just dismantle it if I wanted to."

Raziel smirked. "So, then why aren't you inside?"

"I'm waiting for the right time."

Raziel rolled her eyes and waved to him as she began to close the gates.

Angelus screamed, "Raziel! Wait!"

She held off on closing them completely and asked, "What?"

She watched as Angelus' wings stretched out. His eyes turned completely white, and he began to subtly glow. She looked above her as she heard a creaking sound, as if the barrier were under immense weight. When she looked back at Angelus, she saw how red his face was from the amount of effort that he was radiating.

"You should stop before you pop a blood vessel or strain a wing."

Angelus seemed to take that as a challenge, and she watched as his entire body started to turn bright red from his efforts. Raziel waved again, and she closed the gates. If he was going to succeed, she needed to give herself a slight head start. As she walked across the clearing, she heard a faint sound, as if someone were tapping the glass.

Her stomach began to twist with anxiety, knowing that Angelus was back and could potentially get to her if he wanted to. As she approached her cabin, she had a thought in her head and ringing in her ears, realizing that it was a download.

"He won't get in."

Raziel hadn't experienced it in so long. It felt so foreign to her, and just as soon as she heard that thought, the anxiety in her body seemed to evaporate, and she began to feel safe once more. She was hesitant, but she wanted nothing more than to have a bath. It was such a warm day that a cool bath sounded like the perfect remedy. When she turned the water on, she was relieved to see that it was running clear and thought of when it looked like blood. She shuddered at Angelus' creativity.

Once the tub was filled, Raziel undressed and climbed in as she lowered herself. The cool water felt more refreshing the higher it climbed her body. Once she was settled, Raziel tilted her head back and let her mind wander as she closed her eyes. It was quiet and felt peaceful.

A quick memory of the bonfire from the night before flash in her mind. She was surprised that instead of feeling the immense sorrow that she'd expected, it was replaced with an overwhelming sense of ease. Raziel smiled. She knew that her beloved family would always be with her, giving Nirvana life and filling the atmosphere with love.

When Raziel opened her eyes, Angelus was standing over her, a crazed look on his face as he pushed her head down under the surface. Raziel struggled against him, but it felt like his strength was increasing the further she was under the water. He took his hand off of her, and she sat up, taking deep breaths and gasping.

Raziel looked at him, panicked, and Angelus sneered. "I told you." He walked around the tub, and then said, "Now, I'm due to have a consultation with the general, and I wanted to tell you that I'm going to ensure that you and your sisters lose every drop of your divinity. You're going to suffer once the humans realize what monsters the three of you are."

Raziel shook her head, and she felt her anger start to rise.

She stood up, water pouring off of her, and she stared him straight in the eyes as she asked, "Angelus, why are you doing this? Why me?"

Angelus' pupils widened as he replied, "Torturing you? It's fun."

Raziel shook her head. "No, why did you connect with me the way you did? Why did you put so much effort into getting my attention?"

Angelus smirked. "You were so desperate to experience anything relatively close to love. I smelled your desperation the second I stepped into the forest."

"Angelus, you felt something. I know you did."

Angelus scanned her entire body and looked back up to her eyes. "You were nothing."

Raziel stepped closer to him, and he was forced off the small deck. He kept denying it, but she continued to walk toward him until he stood firmly and forcibly yelled, "Stop!"

Raziel stopped where she was and whispered, "I can sense your nervous energy, Angelus. Stop trying to deny it."

Angelus shook his head. "You're insane."

Suddenly, Raziel felt eerily calm. "No, I've just had enough. You keep threatening me; you keep saying that you're going to kill me. Do it." They stared at each other in silence, and Raziel could see that he was taking it into consideration. When he didn't move, she said, "Then let's go inside."

She took his hand, and he was a bit hesitant. She looked back and said, "Angelus, indulge me one last time."

The two of them went into the cabin, dropped onto the bed, and got lost in each other once more. Raziel had the upper hand, and while he was focused on her curves, she leaned over to reach behind his head and felt the edge of the mattress until she found the handle. As she rocked her body seductively over his, she looked down and saw that he had his eyes shut, giving himself entirely over to her. Raziel pulled the blade from the mattress and waited until it began to glow white. She sat up straight and started to rotate her hips, sending him into pure ecstasy. Raziel then drove the knife deep into his chest cavity, causing Angelus to gasp loudly and look down at the weapon sticking out of him.

He looked up at her, and silver tears began to fall from his eyes as he sputtered, "Raziel."

However, she held a finger up to his lips and whispered, "I think it's best that we see other people."

Angelus' eyes went wide, and as his last breath escaped his lips, a shockwave radiated from his body, sending Raziel flying back. She landed on the floor and groaned in pain. When the pain eased slightly, she stood up and saw the pile of white ashes where Angelus previously was.

She heard a *whooshing* sound behind her, and she casually said, "Natalia."

"What happened here?"

Raziel smirked and looked over her shoulder. "Our little friend had an accident."

Natalia walked over, and she hissed, "You killed *another* angel?!"

Raziel nodded. "I had to."

"Raziel, if you kill one, more will be sent to enact their revenge!"

Raziel's face dropped; she hadn't thought of the repercussions. She looked at Natalia. "He got through the barrier and tried to drown me."

"But did you forget that you're literally immortal, and even if he succeeded, you would resurrect?"

"He made it seem like I would be dead, dead."

Natalia nodded earnestly. "Yes, Raziel. He was a prick, but mind tricks are only just that, tricks." They both looked at the pile behind them, and Natalia sighed. "Azazel has completely lost it. She's started killing her kingdom, and we need to reset her."

"What do we do about *him*?" She pointed to the pile.

Natalia replied, "If you think humans fertilize Nirvana's grounds beautifully, see what divine remains do for you."

Raziel moved past her and grabbed a dustpan, shaking the ashes into it while Natalia watched. She held the dustpan out her front door and allowed the breeze to carry the particles off across the compound. Raziel gleefully watched as the grass became greener. The air also seemed to smell sweeter, and she saw the flowers glow brighter in color. A comforting, warm, and peaceful feeling washed over Raziel. She felt like she could finally, truly, heal from Angelus and the pain that he had caused Nirvana.

When she turned around to go back inside the cabin, Natalia looked at her and impatiently asked, "Are you done now? Can we leave?"

Raziel scoffed. "Oh, I'm sorry. Did my handling of the nuisance in my world really hold us up that long?"

"Yes, Sister. It could have waited."

Raziel rolled her eyes. Natalia was always so keen to look after Azazel that the youngest sister was often forgotten. It was hard not to feel hurt, but Raziel was satisfied knowing that she had taken care of Angelus, on her own, without her sister's interference.

Raziel snidely asked, "Do you mind if I change first?"

Natalia smiled, and with an underlying venom that only an older sister can manage, she said, "I thought you'd never ask. I'll wait for you outside."

After Natalia left the cabin, Raziel turned her attention to her closet and picked out a dress from the very back. It was pink silk and hung on her curves beautifully; the delicate straps that rested on her shoulders led to the tie-up details on the back of the dress. It was one of her favorite pieces to wear, but she rarely had events where she could wear it. Raziel went on to clip her luscious locks on top of her head and allowed a few strands to fall around her face. Deciding to go barefoot felt right, and she knew that it was the best way to connect with the earth beneath her and allow her to have the freedom to ground herself if needed.

As she stepped out of her home, Natalia turned around, and her expression softened. "Ah, what a perfect outfit. Beautiful!"

Raziel blushed from Natalia's unexpected praise. Natalia slightly cleared her throat and asked, "Sister, how did you manage to kill our little problem?"

Raziel quietly said, "I had a blade secured to my mattress."

"And was this something you've always had so accessible?"

Raziel paused for a moment. "Yes, since I started Nirvana. I was scared we may lose our divinity the longer we were here, and I wanted to be able to defend myself if needed."

"Smart, and it clearly proved its use." Natalia extended her hand to Raziel, who took it, and the two of them started to walk through the clearing.

In the blink of an eye, they were inside of Azazel's kingdom. The streets were empty, and they exchanged looks; the domain felt dark and heavy. Natalia sighed, and Raziel started to storm up to the palace. As she tried to walk through the gates, she was pushed back by a force. She staggered backwards and looked over her shoulder to see Natalia's fuming expression.

Natalia shook her head. "It seems that our sweet sister doesn't want visitors."

Raziel felt a deep rage inside of her also and replied, "That's too bad."

Raziel walked back to Natalia, who grabbed her hand, and Raziel pointed to the Great Hall as they walked toward the castle once more. This time, they entered the Great Hall and were met with a massacre. Raziel dropped Natalia's hand and placed her own hand over her mouth in horror. It looked like someone had painted the entire room blood red!

Natalia glanced around, and Raziel screamed, "Sister, your bloody tyranny is done! That is enough!"

Azazel paused her feeding and smiled wickedly at her sisters. Once Natalia and Raziel finished surveying the damage that Azazel had done, they found her torture chamber and put her in her bed. The sisters waited for her to wake up once more. They had bound Azazel's arms and legs to her bedframe, and while they waited, they sat in the small sitting area in Azazel's grand bedroom.

Raziel whispered, "What do you think happened?"

Natalia shrugged. "The same thing that always happens. She succumbed to her curse, and she lost herself to her hunger."

Raziel shook her head. "It hasn't been this bad since the very beginning."

Natalia nodded. "I know, but I suppose we were due for something of this caliber. It ties in nicely with the mass extinction that took place at Nirvana. You're not in the position to be judgmental, Sister."

Raziel slumped in her seat ever so slightly. "That was different."

She pouted, and Natalia lifted her brows. "Was it? How so? Both of your kingdoms were slaughtered because you both can't keep your divinity in check. So please, Sister, do explain how your situation differs."

Raziel stuttered. She was unable to and knew that Natalia was right. She simply whispered, "It won't happen again."

Natalia nodded. "You're right; it *won't* happen again. It seems that I need to be in full control of our powers."

Raziel's mouth dropped open. "I don't think a transfer needs to take place."

Natalia sighed. "I think it might, Sister. I am tired of having to watch over the both of you. I am exhausted from having to clean up your messes when they could've been avoided in the first place. There was no reason, besides your own ignorance, why you couldn't pick up on Angelus' energy. For Heaven's sake, I picked up on it before you did!"

Raziel hated to admit that there was some truth to what Natalia was saying, and her entire community was dead because she was so blinded by Angelus. She felt like she was completely insane by the time she gave her family their final drink. When Raziel thought back to placing her hands on the juice containers, she felt sick to her stomach. She still didn't understand why the only thing that crossed her mind was the word *death*.

"Raziel, snap out of it! It's done and over with. No one is going to come looking for them or for you."

"Natalia, I feel awful. It could have been avoided. I know it could've been. I don't really understand or know where my head was. I don't even really understand how the drinks were filled with that intention."

Natalia sucked air through her teeth. "Have you and Angelus been intimate?"

Raziel looked at the floor, and Natalia stood up. "Right, so I'm assuming that is a yes. That is a power exchange; you allowed him to know the deepest parts of you and gave your-self over to him completely. He was able to put a—we'll call it a bug—in your system, and it began to drive you insane, whether you wanted to see it or not. Plummeting into the lake, the blood in the bath, the killer mob, all leading up to you killing your own followers. It may have been because of *him*, but you were most certainly at fault for not having more control over yourself."

Raziel bowed slightly, and Natalia continued, "I don't want to speak of this again, Sister. We have to get Azazel back in control of her own divinity so the two of you can transfer them over to me." Raziel tried to object, but Natalia held her hand up. "I will not argue about this; you clearly cannot handle it, and let's be honest, Azazel has *never* been able to control hers." Natalia walked over to the bed. "I promise that when I am in control, I will ensure that both of you are well taken care of and never wanted for anything, divine or mortal." Raziel felt defeated but knew that, maybe, it was the right thing to do until they could get a grip on themselves. Natalia sighed. "Honestly, you both are immortal beings and seem to lack the knowledge or control to act as such."

Raziel remained silent, and Natalia walked over to her and leaned forward. "You may be angry with me right now, Sister, but we cannot afford to alert more humans about our presence. They always find a way to kill the divine, and I will not allow that to happen to us." Raziel nodded, but Natalia pushed harder. "I want to hear you say that you will transfer your powers over to me when we reset Azazel." Raziel sighed, and Natalia grabbed her arm, digging her nails deeper into her skin. "Sister, I *need* to hear you say it."

Raziel gasped, and she whispered, "Sister, I don't know. There might be some good to it, but that may be too much power for one of us."

Natalia dug her nails in even deeper. "Sister, I want you to say it."

Raziel looked up at her sister's eyes and saw how unhinged she looked at that moment.

Raziel quietly said, "I will transfer my powers to you once we get Azazel reset and healthy once more."

Natalia nodded and released Raziel's arm. "Good."

They heard a commotion coming from the bed and saw Azazel starting to struggle. Raziel stood up, and as they walked over to the bed, Azazel let out a high-pitched scream.

Natalia tapped her fingers on the edge of the bed. "It seems like you have been quite busy, Sister."

Azazel rolled her eyes and replied, "Big deal, they're just humans. They breed like rats, and my kingdom shall be over-populated once more in a few years."

Raziel was shocked by how her sisters talked about the humans. It was as if they never took the time to get to know them or find out how wonderful they could be.

15

zazel had a crazed look in her eyes, and she looked from Natalia to Raziel and motioned to Raziel with her chin. "What'd you do?" Raziel groaned, and Azazel began to cackle. "You killed your followers."

Raziel and Natalia exchanged looks, and Raziel quietly said, "Unintentionally."

Azazel laughed. "You're going to go down in history as one of the worst cult leaders ever, Raziel."

The term made Raziel flinch. "I wouldn't call myself a cult leader."

Azazel radiated with smugness. "No kidding." She looked

at Natalia, and she faked a pout. "Big bad Natalia, here to save the day once more."

Natalia exhaled loudly. "Azazel."

"Are you going to beg me to control myself again, Sister?"

Natalia shook her head. "No, the two of you are going to transfer your powers over to me, and I will regulate them, so we don't have to go through this process ever again."

Azazel scoffed and looked between them. "There is *no way* that I will *ever* transfer my powers over to *anyone*, and you're absolutely *insane* if you think there is."

Raziel walked over and sat on the bed next to Azazel. She quietly said, "I think it might be the best thing, Azazel. I think it's the only solution before the humans truly catch on to what's going on."

Azazel slowly looked at Raziel and spat at her. "You're a *pathetic* excuse for a divine being; you always have been!"

Natalia walked over, slapped Azazel across the face, and seethed. "If you would've been able to control your hunger, we wouldn't be here, and you wouldn't be facing a tremendous loss." Azazel gave Natalia a nasty glare. "Raziel killed an angel. Now it's only a matter of time before the divine cavalry is called to enact revenge, and frankly, the two of you are so unstable that if I allow either of you to continue with your powers, you will wipe out the entire human race."

Azazel started to laugh loudly. "Oh, Natalia, you say that like it's a bad thing! Look at everything we have witnessed; look at the death, destruction, the hatred! Sister, would it *really* be so bad if all the humans were wiped out?"

Natalia, Raziel, and Azazel all exchanged looks, and Raziel could see that Natalia was genuinely considering it.

Raziel coughed. "Natalia!"

Natalia looked at her and sighed. "Azazel, the repercussions."

Azazel shook her head and pulled at her binds; she was

growing wilder by the second. "Think about it, Natalia. Think about how peaceful the world would be if the humans weren't around anymore. We would have so much fun taking them out one by one, or even by the thousands! Think about how much power we would have, and for how long it would satisfy us."

Natalia stared at her, and Raziel interrupted. "You can't be serious."

Natalia stood up straight. "That's enough!"

Azazel whined, "Come on, Natalia. You used to be fun."

Raziel glared at Azazel. "Enough."

Azazel sneered at her. "Oh, yes. The human lover. You don't get a say, Hippie."

Raziel rolled her eyes, and Natalia coughed. "Okay, we get the point."

Azazel pulled harder at her binds, her bed starting to creak.

Natalia shook her head. "Sister, your hunger brings out your ugliest ideas."

Azazel nodded. "Yes, but they make for interesting goals."

Natalia and Raziel exchanged looks, and Raziel firmly said, "Azazel!"

Natalia held her hand up. "Enough of the back and forth. You don't get to say no."

Natalia walked to the side of the bed and crawled up beside Azazel, who was starting to struggle aggressively, and she began to scream, a panicked look on her face. Natalia looked at her in concern and said, "Azazel, you're never going to be without. You can't sleep for another one hundred years. I won't let it happen."

Azazel had so much hate in her voice as she replied, "I would rather sleep for a *thousand* years."

Natalia nodded and whispered, "Well, your punishment is having to watch your kingdom replenish slowly. By the time it's full once more, your hunger will be overwhelming. You will be in excruciating pain. I'll return, and we will hold the most wonderful feast."

Raziel stared at Natalia in disbelief. She stood up and started to walk toward the door.

Natalia called, "Don't go too far, Raziel! I need you next."

Raziel stopped and turned around. She saw how tender Natalia was being, and it caused her to feel anger and jealousy. She stormed back toward the bed and looked at the both of them, unsure of what to say next. Natalia whispered something to Azazel and placed her hand over top of her chest. Raziel watched as Natalia spoke the ancient language of the angels, and soon, Azazel began to glow, and her eyes turned white. The glowing began to intensify and rise from her body.

Natalia leaned forward and raised her hands. The radiant essence traveled into Natalia's hands, causing her to throw her head back as she began to chant faster. She reached out to Raziel and screamed, "Now!" Raziel grabbed her hand and felt her whole body vibrate.

When Raziel looked at their hands, they were glowing white, and she felt hot, and then everything turned dark. When she opened her eyes, Azazel and Natalia were having tea in the sitting area while Raziel had been placed onto the bed.

When Raziel sat up, it felt like she had fallen down a mountain. She heard, "Ah, finally!" Raziel looked over and saw Natalia's smiling face.

Raziel shook her head. "How long have I been out?"

Natalia quickly replied, "A while; you did beautifully, Sister. Your powers truly brought me to an enlightened state."

When Raziel got out of bed, her legs felt weak, and she

leaned back onto the pillows. Azazel stood up and quickly came over. "Sister, let's get some food in you. It'll help."

Raziel looked at Azazel cautiously. "Are you feeling better?"

"Much."

When they reached the sitting area, Natalia had a plate of food waiting for her, and after Raziel began eating, she felt better.

Natalia waited for a bit before she said, "I think it is safe to say that you will experience human needs. But you won't need to worry about anything. I will ensure that you both *always* have the nourishment that you need."

She smiled at Raziel, who had a mouth full of bread and butter. She nodded and asked, "How are you going to know? Are you going to be popping in randomly to see us while you have your own kingdom to run?"

Natalia shook her head. "No, I am so in tune with the both of you. I feel what each of you needs."

Raziel placed her plate beside her and looked Natalia in the eyes. She started thinking about one of the cookies at the far end of the table, refusing to look at them. Natalia smiled and leaned over to grab a cookie with lemon curd in the middle, the exact one that Raziel was craving. She took it from Natalia and began to greedily eat it.

Natalia grinned and said, "We are going to help Azazel clean up, and then we are going to return to Nirvana."

Raziel nodded and continued to eat off the plate, happily looking from Natalia to Azazel. After they had eaten their fill, they went to clean up the Great Hall.

It took them several months to get the chamber taken apart, clean up the Great Hall, and start to replace the humans in Azazel's care. By the time they were comfortable leaving Azazel's kingdom, a year had passed, and Raziel felt light-hearted and comfortable leaving Azazel.

Over the past year, Azazel had been caring, kind, and a version of herself that Raziel hadn't seen since they were in servitude to Heaven. Raziel loved being able to reconnect with her sisters, and hoped that they would be able to continue down the path that they were starting to forge as they rebuilt Azazel's kingdom.

On the last day, they were all sitting in Azazel's room, and Raziel noticed that the longer they sat there, the more Azazel's face fell… until Raziel couldn't ignore it any longer. She grabbed Azazel's hand and asked, "Sister, what's wrong?"

Azazel shyly replied, "I miss Mulligan. I truly feel awful for the way that I ended things for him."

Raziel looked at Natalia, and Natalia grinned. "I might be able to do something about that."

Azazel's face lit up. "Really?"

Natalia replied, "Perhaps. I don't want you to get your hopes up, but I do feel an excess of energy, and with all of our powers, I think I might be able to come up with a solution."

Azazel gripped Raziel's hand tighter. "Whatever you can do, Sister. I will be so grateful."

Natalia smiled at her sisters and got up to leave the room. Azazel watched her leave in confusion, and Raziel started to ask her questions about her new plans for the kingdom. Azazel excitedly explained the new gardens that she wanted to plant to honor the kingdom's fallen, and wanted the arena where she held The Cunning to be torn down. Raziel felt optimistic and hopeful that Azazel would be able to control herself, now that Natalia was sole the power source.

They talked about the type of flowers that Azazel was thinking of, but were soon interrupted by the door opening. Natalia walked through and had a triumphant look on her face.

She was completely in the room when she looked back and quietly said, "It's alright."

Suddenly, Mulligan walked through the door, much to Azazel's surprise, who jumped up and screamed, startling him. She rushed over and hugged him tightly. Raziel could hear her sobbing and sniffling from her place on the couch.

When Azazel pulled away from him, she desperately said, "I am so sorry, Mulligan."

He had a shocked expression on his face and looked at Natalia, who nodded encouragingly at him. He looked down at the ground and replied, "It's okay, Goddess. I understand."

Azazel's face turned dark as she insisted, "Mulligan! I want you to be angry with me. I deserve it. I slaughtered the entire kingdom. I want you to be *angry* with me!"

He looked up at her cautiously and shook his head. "There is no point in living with the anger, Goddess. I'd rather we just start over."

Azazel's face broke into a smile, and she hugged him again. "I would love that, Mulligan. Until we have a full kingdom and staff again, I want you to be at my side. I don't want you to lift a finger. We are going to do this together."

Raziel and Natalia exchanged looks, and Mulligan sighed. "I would love that."

Azazel nodded. "Good! Good. Now, you're to call me Azazel, and once we have a full staff again, you will assume your position of power, and I expect you to never lift a finger again in servitude."

Mulligan nodded and replied, "Thank you, Azazel."

The two hugged once more, and Raziel couldn't help but be touched by the interaction. She became hopeful that perhaps Natalia would be able to resurrect Ramona, and she looked forward to returning to Nirvana.

When Natalia and Raziel decided that it was time to leave, Azazel held onto them for a considerable amount of time before she let them go. Natalia grabbed Raziel's hand, and they walked through the barrier.

Once they got to the other side of it, they were in the overgrown clearing of Nirvana. Nature had started to take over the compound, the walls were beginning to grow moss, and the grass was up to their knees. The wildflowers were abundant, and fat bumblebees made their way from one flower to the next. Raziel looked around and felt empty.

Natalia gripped her hand and reassured her, "We are going to get it back to its glory."

Raziel shook her head. "I think it's beautiful."

"Yes, but it's inhabitable for the humans whom you want to take care of."

Raziel couldn't help but agree, and they spent another year returning Nirvana back to its prime. The gardens were overflowing with abundance, the grass was greener, and the wildflowers were free to grow as much as they wanted.

After they had cleaned up the cabins, Natalia looked around the compound and said, "This really is a beautiful place, Sister. I see why you love it so much."

"It's even better when it is full of laughter."

Natalia smiled at her. "Ninety-eight more years, Sister. It will fly by. I promise."

Raziel nodded. "Maybe, or it might drag on frightfully slow."

"What can I do for you, Sister?"

Raziel sighed and knew that the moment had come. "You brought Mulligan back for Azazel. I miss Ramona." She trailed off, and a sad look overcame Natalia.

"It was easier to bring Mulligan back because he was still so fresh, Sister. It has been years since Ramona was buried beneath the earth. It's impossible at this point."

Raziel shivered and felt the hot tears threatening to overflow her eyes.

Natalia softly said, "Perhaps you can use this time to reflect on how you want to change things. Maybe instead of trying to interfere with their free-thinking, listen to them."

Raziel grinned. It made sense, and she knew that her leadership skills would need to be evaluated. She looked at Natalia and said, "I like this version of you, Sister."

"I feel a lot better; your energy gave me a new sense of gratitude that I'd never felt before. I felt hollow before, almost empty." Natalia hugged her sister and whispered, "I'll see you soon."

Raziel watched her leave, and when she turned back to Nirvana, she felt hope for the first time in a long time.

16

Ninety-Eight Years Later...

aziel rushed to the gates. She heard the thunderous chatter on the other side of them and was more than ready to welcome her newest family members. As the gates opened, Raziel smoothed her hair and looked around to ensure that everything was perfect. The crowd poured in and circled around her, speaking out their affirmations of love and gratitude.

As everyone entered and stopped around her, waiting for her to speak, Raziel knew precisely where she wanted to start. She looked around at the new faces and loudly said,

"Welcome, everyone. I am so glad that you have all found your way to Nirvana. May we all find peace, love, and true ascension." The group burst into applause, and Raziel continued, "Now, before we all get settled in, there are rules that we all must follow in order to keep Nirvana healthy. The first rule is that everyone must pull their weight. Whatever skills you have, we will find a position for you. The second is that this is a free-loving environment; monogamy, polyamory, or any kind of love is strongly encouraged." Murmurs traveled through the crowd, and Raziel smiled radiantly as she tried to make eye contact with everyone whom she possibly could.

Three years ago, she put out a rumor that the rainforest community was opening up. The old Nirvana had died, and with it, the negativity. Raziel had spent the last years growing and becoming the best version of herself. She had reached her highest level of ascension and was eager to put her newfound skills to use.

As she crossed the clearing, watching people go off into the cabins, she was approached by a small-framed man with shaggy brown hair and wild eyes. Raziel felt an odd feeling as he got closer, and he held his hand out and introduced himself as Charlie. Raziel smiled and asked him what he was looking for in Nirvana, to which he replied, "Inspiration."

"I think you will find plenty of that here."

Charlie bowed and held his hands up in prayer, thanking her.

As the days went on, more people came in from the outside world. Raziel felt excitement and spent her days happier than she had been in years. As people tried to get close to her, she had to keep them at arm's length. Raziel came to the conclusion that she couldn't let anyone into her inner sanctum. She needed to have boundaries, but also be approachable.

Raziel kept the gates open for a week to allow anyone who wanted to enter to come in. She was particularly taken by a man who was a talented Gospel speaker and went by the name of Jim. He didn't stay long, but while he was at Nirvana, he made a significant impact. And after his appearance, several people left with him.

Raziel was sad to see people leave so quickly, but she couldn't deny that he was persuasive and confident in his abilities. Charlie and a small group of girls left the compound about a year after the gates opened, and while Raziel was sad to see more of her followers leave, she was happy that the weird energy that both Charlie and Jim gave off went with them.

After some time, Nirvana fell into a comfortable routine. Everyone knew their place in the community, they respected each other and her as their leader, and for a while, Raziel forgot about her sisters and what had happened.

After a lust-filled full moon ritual, Raziel walked to her cabin and was surprised to see Natalia sitting on her bed. She gasped and ran to Natalia's open arms.

"Natalia! It's so nice to see you."

"Sister, Nirvana is thriving!"

Raziel nodded. "It's become everything I ever wanted." Natalia beamed, and Raziel saw how radiant she appeared, but she could sense that something was off. She asked, "What's going on?"

Natalia sighed. "I felt a shift last week. I wasn't sure if it was anything serious, but I felt it again today, intensely."

"Well, it's nothing you can't handle, right? You have all the powers you could ever need."

Natalia sighed again. "I haven't felt as connected to the powers in years, almost eighty years at this point."

"You went eighty years with mine and Azazel's powers dormant?"

Natalia nodded, and Raziel started to panic. She knew that the powers needed to be used consistently, or they could die out, and it would cause the user to divinely implode.

Natalia picked up on Raziel's thoughts, and she continued, "Which brings me to why I am here. I need to offload some of your powers back to you."

Raziel shook her head. "Sister, I can't. I am so scared of what could happen."

"Raziel, I know you can handle them. They are *your* powers. They were *made* for you, and you're the only one who can bring out their full potential if something goes wrong."

Raziel was quiet for a moment, and then she asked, "Have you seen Azazel yet?"

Natalia went silent, and tension formed between them.

Raziel cautiously asked, "What?"

Natalia cleared her throat. "Azazel's hunger has returned."

"What happened?!"

Natalia looked down. "Azazel killed Mulligan again."

"How is that possible?"

Natalia looked up and quietly answered, "I'm not sure, but she only lasted twenty years." Raziel was shocked. Natalia whispered, "I'm proud of you, Sister. Truly. Nirvana is beautiful, and you seem to be doing well."

She held out her hand. As Raziel touched her fingers, their hands began to glow. Raziel felt warm, and the emptiness inside of her was filled.

Raziel pulled her hand away, and Natalia said, "There is just one thing. You still won't be able to feel the love that you want so badly."

Raziel nodded. "I understand."

"I am going to hold on to Azazel's powers for a while longer. I have lulled her into a deep slumber and will awaken her when I deem her ready."

Raziel observed her feet, and Natalia said loudly, "Speak."

Raziel sighed. "I don't think she should *ever* get her powers back, Sister. How many times do we need to go through this?"

Natalia's expression hardened. "Eventually, I will have to, correct?"

Raziel agreed and continued, "How many times do we have to paint over blood, tear down a torture chamber, and babysit her?"

Natalia said harshly, "I need to put her powers *somewhere*."

Raziel looked up. "I can host them until you are ready to wake her."

Natalia studied her face. "I will leave them with you tonight, if you are ready." Raziel had a look of surprise, and Natalia explained, "I don't know if what I felt was another angel, but if it was, you are the most exposed. I want you to be as protected as possible."

Raziel felt a wave of excitement wash over her, and she held her hand out to Natalia once more. When Natalia grabbed it, her fingers were ice cold, and it spread through Raziel's entire body. She shuddered, and finally, Natalia let go of her hand. Raziel felt electric; she shuddered, and Natalia had a serious look on her face.

"You will eventually feel her hunger. It is quite intoxicating and painful. You *must* resist it, Sister."

Raziel nodded. "How long are you going to keep her asleep?"

Natalia sighed. "Five hundred years."

Raziel couldn't believe what she was hearing. "That long?"

Natalia nodded. "She is a danger to everyone."

Raziel couldn't help but agree; Azazel *had* always been a liability.

Natalia exhaled. "I feel much better. I will come back to

check on you soon. Keep a lookout for anything out of the ordinary."

Natalia quickly turned and melted into the shadows. Raziel felt delicious. A tingle went up her spine, she was covered in goosebumps, and she felt like she was buzzing. She walked over to her bed and threw herself onto it. It wasn't long before Raziel drifted off to sleep, where she dreamt of broken scenes, absorbing different human life essences. She went through countless humans before she got the wicked idea to drink from them, and the next humans she killed, she bit deep into their necks, drinking the warm, coppery blood that flowed freely from their bodies.

Raziel opened her eyes as the sun washed over her. She felt a deep hunger, thinking that she was just feeling the effects of the ritual from the night before and the power exchange with Natalia. She figured that her body finally caught up.

Raziel quickly got dressed and ran to the dining hall, where they were dishing out thick pancakes. She requested double servings, and they happily obliged. Raziel sat at the table closest to the door and began to tuck in, every bite satisfying her for a second before she became famished once more.

Once the hall cleared, Raziel walked up and asked for all of the leftovers to be brought to her table. The kitchen crew brought trays over one by one and set them down in front of her. Raziel began shoveling food into her mouth as if she hadn't eaten in months.

She emptied all the trays, and when she took the last bite, the hunger seemed to only deepen. Raziel tapped her fingers on the table and looked around. A sweet smell swept through the dining hall, and she got up to follow it.

When she got to the kitchen, she saw the staff baking cookies. They greeted her excitedly, and the chef, John, asked if she wanted to taste what they were making. She agreed and took an entire tray from them, causing the staff to exchange concerned looks. Raziel thanked them and carried the tray out the door.

She walked down to her cabin, and when she was behind the closed door, she shoved three cookies at once into her mouth until she finished the entire tray. Raziel looked at the tray until it went fuzzy. She didn't think she would feel Azazel's hunger so quickly; she didn't know how her sister had dealt with it for so long.

She called out, "Natalia!" Hoping that her sister would hear her, Raziel waited for several minutes, and when her sister didn't appear, she called out to her again.

Raziel felt like her stomach was going to rip itself apart. She screamed for her sister, and finally, heard the familiar *whooshing* sound.

Natalia asked, "Already?"

Raziel nodded. Natalia sighed and looked out the window. "Sister, which member irritates you the most?"

Raziel shook her head. "None of them. I love them all."

Natalia smirked. "Impossible! Humans can be so irritating. It's okay to sacrifice one. It's not the same level that Azazel did; it's one. I will condone it."

Raziel groaned. "Pick one of the men."

Natalia sneered. "Sister, I like your choice."

Natalia left the cabin and returned a short while later with one of the cabin builders. Raziel knew that he agitated most people in the compound; he was smug and slightly ignorant. He wouldn't be missed in the grand scheme of things.

When he was brought in, Raziel tilted her head in interest, and without looking away from him, she said, "Leave us."

Natalia bowed and backed out of the cabin. Raziel smirked at him and asked, "Your name is Kurtis, right?" He nodded, and she took a step closer to him. "Have you been enjoying your time here in Nirvana, Kurtis?"

She cooed his name, and he smiled wide. "Yeah, it's been super awesome, but I've been told that I make it better."

Raziel scoffed. "Ah, there it is."

Kurtis looked confused, and before he could object, Raziel placed her hands on his chest, pushing him to the ground; he was shocked by her strength. Raziel crawled on top of him, her hands beginning to glow. She watched as a tiny glowing faint ball came up between Kurtis' lips. She leaned down and inhaled the ball, her entire body feeling replenished, and her hunger subsided ever so slightly. Kurtis' body began to wither beneath her, his cheeks sunken in, his eyes became dark sockets, and his bones began to protrude from his skin.

Natalia opened the door and looked at the corpse beneath Raziel, and asked, "Feel better?"

Raziel looked up and said, "One more."

Natalia nodded and repeated, "One more."

Raziel turned her attention back to Kurtis. She knew he would make beautiful compost and would bury him later. She stood up and walked over to her bed. Flashes of her dream from the previous night popped into her head, and a wicked grin came across her face as the door opened to another builder.

The first thing he did was look at Kurtis on the floor. He viciously shook his head and yelled, "No!" as Raziel rushed toward him, and Natalia pulled the door shut behind him.

Raziel was feral. She grabbed him by the throat and started to dig her nails in until they began to draw blood. Her mouth watered, and she whispered, "Now, now, builder. That's enough out of you."

Raziel threw him onto the floor, and he tried to claw himself away, but Raziel pulled his legs, flipped him over, and sat on his chest. She placed both hands on his chest. "Now, you're going to cooperate, or I promise I will make it as painful as possible for you."

The builder nodded, and as Raziel leaned down to lick the blood off of his neck, he groaned in pain. He tasted sweet, and she couldn't help what happened next. Raziel bit into his neck, causing him to cry out. She bit in deeper as his blood flowed out around her mouth. Raziel saw the faint glow out of the corner of her eye. She felt the blood rush out of her mouth as she sat up to absorb the glow. She bent down and surrounded her mouth around the orb, and similar to what happened to Kurtis, the man withered away to nothing.

Natalia came back into the cabin, and Raziel smiled at her. "I'm full."

Natalia nodded and asked, "What are we going to do with them?"

Raziel wiped her mouth with her arm. "Rose garden."

Natalia scoffed. "You're so predictable."

This caused Raziel to shrug. "Maybe, but my flowers always look the best when they are being nourished by humans."

They picked up the corpses and walked out the back of the cabin, dropped them onto the ground, and began to separate one of the most enormous rose bushes.

Once they had dug a big enough hole, they pushed the two bodies in and placed the flowers over top of them. When the bodies were covered up, Natalia looked around the garden and whispered, "They really *are* immaculate, Sister." Raziel nodded. They locked eyes, and a concerned Natalia asked, "Are you going to be okay if I leave?"

Raziel paused. "I think so. I didn't think it would overtake me so quickly." Natalia agreed, and Raziel continued, "I think I will be satisfied for some time now."

Natalia replied, "I hope so. I can't authorize you to kill any more humans. You're trying to rebrand Nirvana."

Raziel sighed; she still had to think of a story to tell the rest of the commune when they realized that Kurtis and the other man were missing. Raziel's eyes went wide as she remembered that she didn't even get to know the other man's name.

She groaned. "Natalia, that was awful. I wasn't… divine; I was some horrific monster."

Natalia smiled and replied, "It's such a wicked thing, isn't it?" Raziel nodded, and Natalia added, "But the rush?"

Raziel looked up at her quickly. "It's something I have never experienced before."

"It makes sense why Azazel was willing to risk her entire kingdom for the feeling." Natalia pointed at Raziel. "You need to fight it longer, figure out how to hone it until it is transferred back to Azazel. No more deaths, Raziel. I mean it."

Raziel's face fell into a pout as she whispered, "Fine."

As Natalia walked past her, she asked, "Have you noticed anything?"

Raziel shook her head. "Nothing besides my new feelings."

"Keep your eyes open."

Raziel gripped her sister's hand and squeezed it. "Thank you for helping me."

Natalia smiled and pulled her hand away as she walked back into the smallest shadows of the cabin. Raziel waited until the coast was clear and walked through her cabin. As she caught a glimpse of herself in the mirror, she saw that she was still covered in blood. It set something primal off in her brain. Raziel walked out the front door and up to the dining hall, requesting that the kitchen staff make a large batch of jungle juice.

The kitchen staff rushed to her, asking if she was okay. In a monotone voice, Raziel told them she had just injured herself doing some gardening but was alright. She told them in a commanding tone to make the juice quickly.

When she walked out of the dining hall, Raziel walked over and rang the bell to signal a community meeting. People started to fill out the space in front of her. Raziel held her arms up and loudly said, "Everyone, circle around me. Don't be shy. Get close."

The members all stepped close to her, and the kitchen staff brought out a large pitcher of jungle juice. Raziel smirked and loudly said, "Would you be able to find me a chalice in the kitchen?"

One of the women ran back and returned a second later with a large silver chalice. She handed it over to Raziel, along with the jungle juice pitcher. Raziel poured some of the juice into the chalice, and as the liquid flowed into the cup, she thought about absorbing the other members and how good it would feel.

She then noticed that the liquid turned a bright yellow before returning to the usual dark color that it initially was. Raziel lifted the cup above her head and yelled, "Brothers! Sisters! We are on the verge of making history. I have decided that I want you all to be ingrained into Nirvana's very essence for the rest of time."

There were murmurs of appreciation throughout the crowd. Raziel welcomed them all to begin to drink from the cup. As each person sipped, Raziel made sure to whisper words of encouragement to each and every member. With each person who passed, Raziel grew colder, *hungrier*. As the last family member took a sip, the first few started to foam at the mouth. One by one, they all began to drop to the ground, and eventually, the glowing orbs raised from their mouths, and Raziel held her hands open and summoned them into her.

Raziel felt powerful, and she smirked as the last few orbs made their way into her. She stepped over the bodies, leaving them there to fertilize the ground. She went back to her cabin and washed the blood from her face and neck, then braided her hair into a thick braid that draped over her shoulder.

She then left her cabin and calmly walked over the bodies toward the gates of Nirvana. The gates opened, and the only thing that Raziel wanted was to go into the city. She coolly walked the path through the forest; the animals were quiet, and the breeze had stopped entirely. As she approached the city, Raziel was overwhelmed with *hunger*. She continued to walk into the city, soon realizing that the streets were bare. Raziel was starting to feel a sense of desperation without any humans in sight.

She stopped in front of a building that had hundreds of windows. She walked inside and saw a woman behind a desk. Raziel smirked as the woman welcomed her and said that she was at one of the city's hotels. Raziel didn't catch the name of the hotel. She was too focused on the sound of blood flowing through the woman's arteries. It made Raziel's mouth water, and she felt the hunger starting to take over her entire body once more.

She asked the woman to grab a map of the city. As the woman turned around, Raziel jumped over the desk, dragging the woman to the ground. When Raziel bit into her, she started to cough and retch in disgust.

Raziel backed away from the woman and screamed, "What's wrong with you?!"

The woman whimpered, "I'm sick."

Raziel spat at her and roared, "You are vile!"

She went over and snapped the woman's neck. When the

orb flew out of her mouth, Raziel allowed it to float up into the air until it disappeared. She got up and left the hotel, and she started to run down the street.

Raziel felt like a wild animal on the hunt. Her latest victim wasn't worthy of being absorbed, and she *hated* it. Her ears began to ring, causing her to stop, and she looked around. There was no one around her, but she felt like she wasn't alone. Raziel continued walking down the street and smelled the sweet scent of baked goods.

She followed it until she came to a small bakery. The shop was filled with several bakers and customers, and Raziel felt herself salivating. When she walked in, she locked the door behind her, bringing attention to herself.

Raziel held her hands up and calmly said, "You are all so lucky that I am here to relieve you of your humanity."

The humans all exchanged looks, and a woman with a piece of cake in her hands chuckled, "I don't know what you've been smoking, but you've got to give me the number!"

Raziel stared at her and sneered. "You're first."

She walked over to the woman and grabbed her by the neck. The sheer force of her grip crushed the woman's throat, and the glowing orb instantly flew out of her mouth. Raziel inhaled it, and it caused the other people inside the bakery to panic.

Raziel looked around and loudly stated, "There is no need for fear. Come to me, my children. You shall be blessed for all of eternity." The humans began to cry as they cowered in the corner. Raziel walked over to them and said, "Be not afraid. You're going to be a part of history, of something so much bigger than you could ever begin to imagine. Die with dignity, and I will ensure that you'll never be forgotten." She stared at all of them and motioned. "Who's next?"

A large man stood up and lifted his head slightly. Raziel

smirked and whispered, "Brother, welcome home." The man grabbed her hands, and Raziel said, "Please, lie down."

He did so, and she climbed on top of his chest. She absorbed him, followed by the others, until there was only a small pile of corpses left on the floor.

Raziel went through every single building in the city until she had absorbed every human. After the last, Raziel started to slowly walk back to Nirvana. She allowed her fingers to run through the fauna, and the sun was peeking through the trees, casting beams through the branches. It was beautiful. Raziel felt like she was on top of the world.

As she walked through the gates of Nirvana, she felt comfortable and relieved to be home. Walking past the pile of her followers, Raziel smirked, knowing that they would be a part of her for the rest of eternity. When the lake came into view, she decided that a refreshing dip would be the *perfect* way to end her day.

She stripped down and slowly walked into the lake. The water was refreshing, and she felt tingles all over her body. Dipping her head under the surface of the water, Raziel had flashbacks of the absorptions that she had just completed, and her heart felt elated. She finally understood why Azazel was always angry and wanted to keep humans as livestock.

When she came back up, something felt off. She looked around and felt like something had changed; she felt like she was being watched. Raziel wiped her eyes and felt exposed all of a sudden. She slowly swam over to leave the lake. With every step she took, a feeling of dread became increasingly overwhelming, and she felt like her lungs were being squeezed. Raziel dropped to her knees, and as the water dripped off her body, it felt as if she were being licked by the hottest flames.

As quickly as the feelings started, they stopped, and Raziel glanced around. Nirvana was utterly empty. She stood up and walked toward her cabin. As she opened the door, a very disheveled Natalia was crawling across her floor. Raziel gasped and ran over to her.

Natalia looked up and weakly whispered, "They're here."

Raziel shook her head, not understanding.

Natalia gasped, "The high council. They found Azazel."

Raziel's eyes grew wide. The high council was the highest tier of angels in Heaven, and they doled out punishment and justice; they were right below the Creator himself.

A sense of nervousness overcame Raziel, and she desperately asked, "Natalia, what happened?" She helped her sister up onto the bed.

Natalia continued to tell Raziel that she had been at Azazel's kingdom, checking on her. She had been in Azazel's bedroom when the doors flew open, and six white-robed angels came flying in. They tried to grab Natalia, but she had shrunk into the shadows as they circled Azazel's body.

"They are coming for us," Natalia warned.

Raziel paced in front of Natalia. She cursed under her breath and said, "Sister, if they come here—"

Natalia shook her head. "Not if. It's *when* they get here."

"Sister, I have done something."

Natalia tilted her head and quietly said, "Oh, Raziel. No."

Raziel nodded. "I couldn't help it, Natalia. The hunger was excruciating."

Natalia became livid, and when she tried to stand up, she felt weak and had to sit back down. She glared at Raziel. "How many?"

Raziel refused to look her in the eyes, and Natalia screamed, "Raziel! How many humans did you kill?"

Raziel looked up and said, "The entire commune, and the whole city."

Natalia whispered, "The entire city, Raziel?" She nodded,

and Natalia gripped the bridge of her nose. "Raziel, how could you?"

Raziel became angry and hissed, "It is the *worst* pain that I have ever felt. I needed to satisfy it. I felt like it was going to destroy me."

Natalia seethed. "You speak as if I have never felt it, experienced it." Raziel stared at her. "I'm aware of how awful it is, Raziel. I'm aware, yet I didn't go on a massive killing spree because of it. Do you realize that because of you and Azazel not being able to control your basic primal needs, you have both alerted them to where we are?" Raziel remained silent, and Natalia screamed, "They are going to capture us, and we are going to be brought in front of the Creator. Judgment will be dished out, and we will have *nowhere* else to go."

As Natalia finished her sentence, the door of the cabin flew open, and six white-robed figures were standing in the doorway. Raziel stared in shock and screamed with such force that the windows in the cabin shattered.

Natalia faintly whispered, "Raziel, stop. We need to go."

Desperately, Raziel pleaded, "I need to get dressed first."

The angels stared at her, their eyes milky white, and they all opened their mouths at the same time. A deep voice sounded, "You have been summoned."

Raziel started to panic, and before she could say anything else or reach Natalia, they were transported to an all-black circular room with the six angels surrounding them, sitting on oversized chairs that towered over Raziel, Azazel, and Natalia. When Raziel tried to speak, nothing came out. She patted her throat and tried to scream, but again, silence.

Azazel had been brought out of her slumber and was starting to fully become aware once more. When she tried to speak, it came out as raspy squeaks. Natalia was the only one who was focused and staring forward.

The high council opened their mouths and said as one,

"The fallen have been accused of using mankind as their personal food source. Millions of humans have been slaughtered, precious lives stolen, and they have done *nothing* but be detrimental to the delicate mankind ecosystem."

Raziel and Azazel glanced at each other, and Raziel saw the fear in her eyes as the council continued, "The fallen shall be condemned to the lowest level of the pit. They will be bound for all of eternity, lose their ability to speak and their powers, and the being who houses the hunger shall only know starvation until she withers away to dust."

Raziel started to shake. The pit was in the darkest place of Heaven, and when prisoners were sent there, they were forgotten and perished in the cells. Once the sentence had been issued, Raziel was pulled out of the court, away from Azazel and Natalia. Azazel was the only one who looked at Raziel as she was dragged away.

Raziel was brought to a room with a mattress on the floor, black walls, and no windows. She was to sit in darkness for all of eternity, to be forgotten, and eventually, die. Raziel slumped against the wall and fell to the floor. Her stomach started to grumble. She smirked as she thought of every absorption, every death, and every scream of desperation. Raziel finally agreed with Azazel wholeheartedly. Humans deserved it, and she would *never* feel remorse. Raziel was relieved that there was finally no pressure on her. Eventually, she could slip into the darkness and become nothing more than a legend.

The End

ABOUT THE AUTHOR

Viola Tempest is a dystopian fantasy and paranormal romance author who yearns to expose the truth of those in the modern world: the good, the bad, and the ugly. Her inspiration primarily stems from life experiences, those who annoy her, ex-boyfriends, and the crazy dreams that pop into her head every once in a while.

www.ingramcontent.com/pod-product-compliance
Lightning Source LLC
Chambersburg PA
CBHW021332190726
48288CB00003B/1066